Tales of Hans Christian Andersen

Tales of Hans Christian Andersen

Translated and Introduced by
Naomi Lewis

Illustrated by
Joel Stewart

CANDLEWICK PRESS
CAMBRIDGE, MASSACHUSETTS

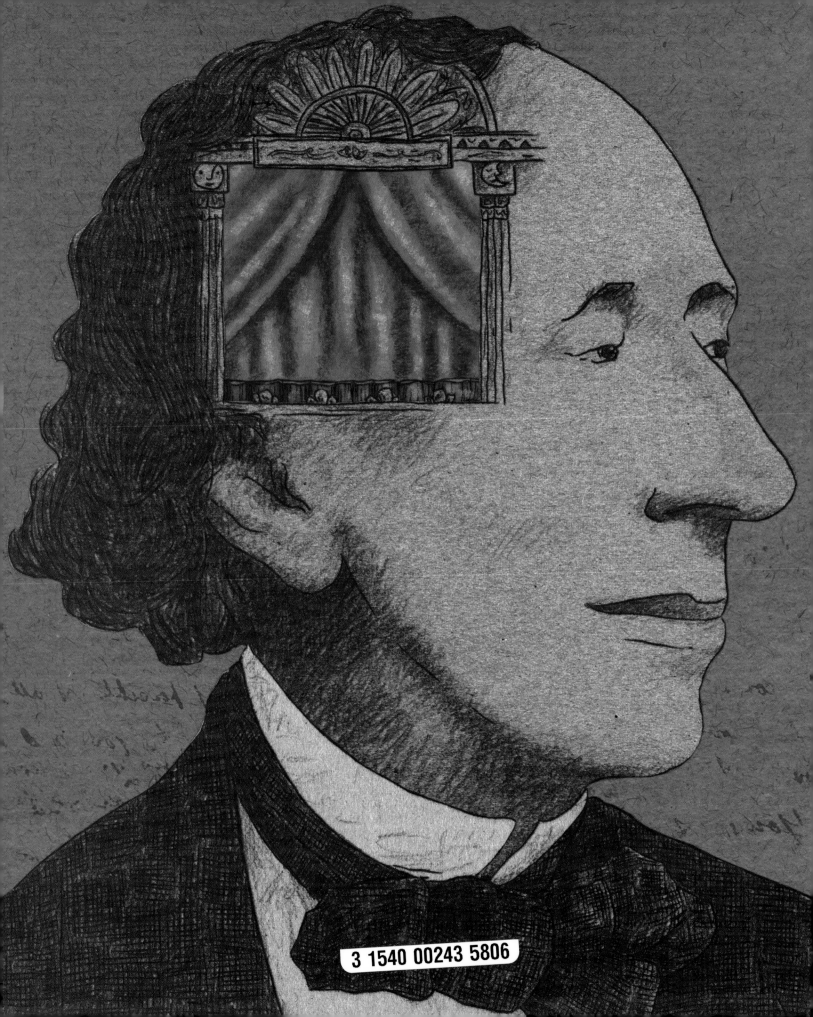

Some say that two fairies, Fairy Nice and Fairy Noxious, came to Andersen's christening. Only two? Well, it was such a poor affair that two seemed quite enough. This transcript has been found.

Fairy Nice:

I give him genius.

Fairy Noxious:

You must be new to this game. He has genius already, poor fellow. Since he's a writer, I give him bad reviews — he'll hate that.

Fairy Nice:

His greatest wish will be fulfilled both in his lifetime and beyond — fame.

Fairy Noxious:

Don't you know anything? Every wish has its price; the greater the wish, the greater the price. For a start, I give him toothache, doubt, and depression. And he'll have no descendants.

Fairy Nice:

No descendants? Nonsense. Wherever stories are read or heard, the Andersen line will live on.

Here the transcript abruptly stops.

*H*ere is Andersen's story.

Hans Christian Andersen (1805–1875) was born in the Danish town of Odense on April 2, two months before his parents' wedding.

An only child, he was loved by both of them, but—poverty apart—his parents had little in common. His mother was a simple, hard-working peasant woman: pious, super-stitious, illiterate. But his father was very different. At twenty-two (several years younger than his wife), he was earning a poor living as a shoemaker and feeling bitter at his lack of education. Yet he was a reader and a thinker, and much ahead of his time in his rebellious views on politics and religion. An original in other ways too, he gave his child the thought that every non-human creature or thing—a leaf, a beetle, a darning needle—has a character of its own: a thought that was to prove invaluable to the later Andersen. Invaluable too was his father's teaching him how to make and work small toy theaters—human life in miniature. But when Andersen was six or so, his father, driven by poverty and depression, left for the wars—to return a sick man. He died when Andersen was eleven.

Young Andersen never played with other children. He was busy enough reading, listening to stories, singing ("a little nightingale"), working his own toy theater and, always, making friends with bookish or theatrical adults. He was sent to school, but at the first sign of harshness or bullying, he would go straight home and never return. The only place he stayed was a small Jewish school where there was no unkindness. Sadly, within a year, it was closed.

6

Even as a boy, Andersen never doubted that greatness — in some field — awaited him, but Odense, his hometown, held no future. The idea of fame that fired his imagination was of no ordinary kind. He must reach its very pinnacle; it must last into unknown time. So, at fourteen, he made his way to Copenhagen.

The golden path to fame was hard to find. For three years, Andersen starved and froze, singing, pleading, clowning his way into likely houses, haunting the theater (would his dream come about through acting?), endlessly scribbling plays. Eventually notice was taken of him. Something had to be done with this unquenchable maverick! Funds were arranged; the formidable Jonas Collin, a leading state councilor, was appointed guardian. Amazing! From gutter level, the waif had leapt into the high professional class. What's more, he had gained a family — including the five teenage Collins (three boys, two girls). But every wish has its price; the boy now had to be educated. He was sent to a school, nearly sixty miles away, with a sadistic headmaster, Simon Meisling. Already seventeen, an awkward, bony scarecrow over six feet tall, in shabby, outgrown clothes, Andersen was put in a class of eleven-year-olds. What's more, Meisling forbade him all freedom, including the writing of poetry. It was the hardest period of Andersen's life. But at last, with the exams somehow behind him, he could choose his profession. No problem: he would write. Soon he was a known author of adult poems, plays, travel writing, a successful first novel. And yet, and yet, had he found the path to everlasting fame? In the New Year of 1835, he was deep in a new project — fairy tales, told in a personal way. By May, a thin paperbound booklet of four of these stories was on sale. It was the first sound of a wholly original voice.

Some sour Danish critics, who never forgave the author's "low" beginnings, condemned the tales for lacking a moral, for their conversational (non-classical) style, and for the absurdity of giving speech to objects. Yet these daring novelties were the stories' particular assets. The increasing praise from children, adults, leading critics, and fellow writers gave fuel to Andersen's invention. He had no need for other people's ideas. As his father once had shown him, stories lay all around — in an old trunk, a toy, a bundle of matches. It was his fellow writers everywhere who most quickly recognized the invention in Andersen's creative genius, the range that he was adding to the craft. Masters themselves, they greeted him as a master.

Andersen called his life a fairy tale. True enough. The magic of genius would propel a penniless provincial slum boy to extraordinary fame. But fairy tales also have their darker side — terrible trials, forests of thorns, unscalable glass mountains. There were many trials in Andersen's life. It was years before conventional Danes allowed him to forget his pitiful origins, a rejection that shook his confidence almost to the end of his life. Abroad he had no such difficulties.

He never married. The idea seemed pleasant enough, but not very real. In earlier days, he argued that he was "too ugly." Later his craggy looks would acquire (as abundant photographs show) a striking distinction. Also, for years he had no sure income. He never even had a home of his own. (How could he fit in his increasing passion for travel if he was tied to a home?) Andersen knew himself to be an outsider, a loner, an observer; his gift required him to be so. The trappings of a conventional life would have held him back.

As a dinner guest, he could charm, he could entertain. Even the royal heads of the many small kingdoms of nineteenth-century Europe sought and enjoyed his company and his tales;

the actor star of his early dreams was never far below the surface. When he read his stories aloud, he could hold spellbound an overflowing hall of workmen, a royal court — children, too, of course. You can still hear his beguiling speaking voice in the printed text.

Yet behind the confident performer lay someone racked with self-doubt. He would fill his diary with self-pity, self-blame, and self-mockery. Yes, he had toothache, too. But in his published work, he could free himself — there is scarcely a page, whatever its gloom, that is not suddenly lit by his underplayed, irresistible humor. In company Andersen always concealed his self-doubts, but he left clues to his private world throughout the tales. In one guise or another, perhaps at a fleeting moment, perhaps as a full portrait ("The Ugly Duckling"), he liked to appear in each. Try to track him through the stories in this book. It's an intriguing quest.

Andersen did achieve the improbable golden prize of his life's desire. In his late years, the Danes themselves, once so cold toward "the washerwoman's crazy son," showered the highest of honors upon him. Two centuries after his birth, he is his nation's icon. And his descendants? Every children's book whose characters are non-human but whose story reflects the range of human behavior is descended from Andersen. Such books — you must know them well — are beyond counting, and more are born daily. Also among Andersen's legion descendants is every invented fairy tale today. As for the great tales in this book, their brilliance is untouched by time. They can be read again and again, each time revealing more — which was always the writer's intention.

Naomi
Lewis

9

For the
Society of
Wonders

J. S.

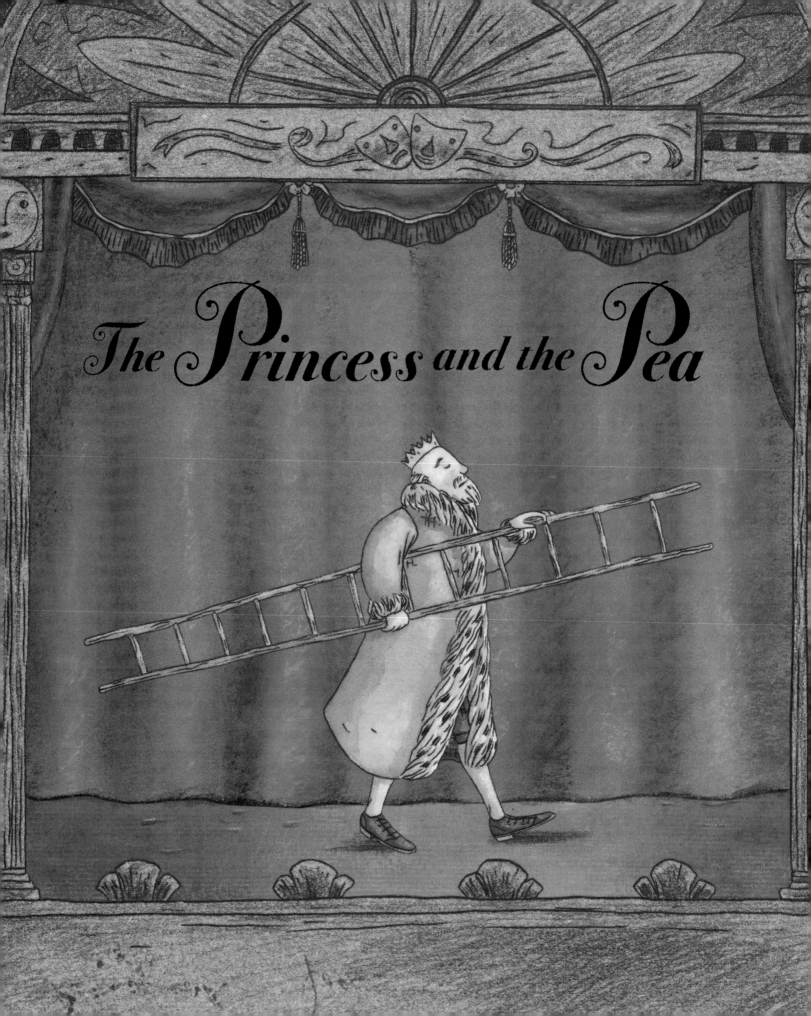

The Princess and the Pea

This has the distinction of being one of the first four "fairy tales" Andersen tried out in May 1835. Would they bring fame, shame, or silence? Well, they brought very strange reviews, for Andersen was known only as an adult writer. Yet fame soon came—and stayed. Though he explained that the idea for this tale may have come from the women telling folktales and fables to each other in the spinning room or the hop fields, the listening boy had now become the skillful artist. Indeed, as our story shows, he was a master from the start. This pioneer tale is a small perfection. Andersen's artful simplicity keeps the tale alive: one pea; a huge load of bedclothes; a royal household where the king answers the door and the queen arranges the bed, yet we have no doubt of their royalty; oh, and that single pea is later sent to a museum.

The first English translators could not understand Andersen's humor or his subtlety. One pea? That was absurd. Three might be more credible. The museum is ignored. Sadly, some of these early versions are still in use. Look out for those rogue peas.

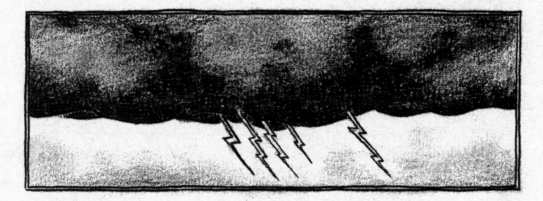

THERE WAS ONCE A PRINCE WHO WISHED to marry a princess—but a real princess she had to be. So he traveled all the world over to find one; yet in every case something was wrong. Princesses there were in plenty, yet he could never be sure that they were the genuine article; there was always something, this or that, that just didn't seem as it should be. At last he came back home, quite downhearted, for he did so want to have a real princess.

One evening there was a fearful storm; thunder raged, lightning flashed, rain poured down in torrents—it was horrifying. In the midst of it all, someone knocked at the palace door, and the old king went to open it.

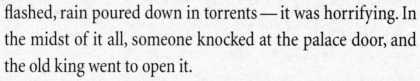

Standing there was a princess. But goodness! What a state she was in! The water ran down her hair and her clothes, through the tips of her shoes, and out at the heels. Still, she *said* she was a real princess.

Well, we'll find out soon enough, the old queen thought. She didn't say a word, though, but went into the spare bedroom, took off all the bedclothes, and laid a small pea on the mattress. Then she piled twenty more mattresses on top of it, and twenty eiderdowns over that. There the princess was to sleep that night.

When morning came, they asked her how she had slept.

"Oh, shockingly! Not a wink of sleep the whole night long! Heaven knows what was in the bed, but I lay on something hard that has made me black-and-blue all over. It was unspeakable."

Now they were sure that here was a real princess, since she had felt the pea through twenty eiderdowns and twenty mattresses. Only a real princess could be so sensitive.

So the prince married her: no need to search any further. The pea was put in a museum; you can go and see it for yourself if no one has taken it.

There's a fine story for you!

The Tinderbox

*B*y chance or design, this was the opening tale of Andersen's trial fairy tale booklet of 1835. So "The Tinderbox" is Story One of Andersen's own count of 156. In most ways it isn't a typical Andersen work at all. Ingredients are quite openly plucked from the Arabian Nights, *from* Grimm, and from other familiar folklore: most obviously the tinderbox ("Aladdin"), the crosses on doors ("Ali Baba"), and the trail of grain ("Hansel and Gretel"). The soldier hero might have stepped out of any stock traditional source. But the telling could come from no other voice. Who else could make every line come so alive? As with his own wishes and desires Andersen made good use of superlatives: the overabundance of coins, the impossible size of the dogs' eyes! The three extraordinary dogs are entirely Andersen's — so obliging in all their tasks, so correct at the end (a wonderful touch) as seated guests at the wedding feast.

Some early Danish critics complained that Andersen's new "fairy tales" had no moral and that the language was not refined, too much like common speech. For the young especially, these points were part of the lure; for later writers, a major gift. To be sure, morality works in odd ways. Is our hero noble? No. Nursery tale heroes rarely are. But given the role, he has the hero's privileges. Does he cheat the witch? Of course. I suspect that children pause a bit more at the cheating than at the lopping off of the witch's head. "The Tinderbox" remains a popular choice for children to this day.

*A*SOLDIER CAME MARCHING DOWN the road — Left, right! Left, right! He had a pack on his back and a sword at his side; he had been in the wars and was now on his way home. Along the road, he met a witch. She was a frightful sight! Her lower lip hung down almost to her waist.

"Hello, young soldier," said the witch. "That's a handsome sword you have, and a fine knapsack, too. You're a proper soldier, and no mistake! Do you want money? I'll show you how to get as much money as you want."

"Thanks very much, old witch," said the soldier.

"Do you see that big tree?" said the witch. She was pointing to a tree just beside them. "It's quite hollow inside. If you climb up to the top of the trunk, you'll see a hole, and you can slide down that to the bottom. I'll tie a rope around your waist so that I can pull you up when you call."

"What am I supposed to do down there?" said the soldier.

"Fetch the money, that's what," said the witch. "Now listen to me. When you get to the bottom, you'll find yourself in a long passage. It will be perfectly light, because more than a hundred lamps are kept burning there. You'll see three

doors; they'll be easy to open because the keys are in the locks. Start in the first room. You'll find a wooden chest in the middle of the floor, with a dog sitting on it. The dog has eyes as big as teacups — but don't let that bother you. Here, I'm giving you my blue-checked apron. Spread it out on the floor, lift the dog onto it — no, don't be afraid — then open the chest and take as much money as you like out of it. It is all coppers, I must tell you. If you'd rather have silver, you must go into the next room. You'll find a dog there with eyes as big as millstones, but don't let that worry you. Just lift the dog, put it on the apron, and help yourself. If it's gold you are after, though, you can get that in the third room, as much as you can carry. But the dog there has eyes as big as the Round Tower. That's a dog of dogs — you won't see his like anywhere else in this world, I can tell you. But never you mind about that. Just put him onto my apron and he won't do you any harm. Then take as much gold as you like."

"That doesn't sound so bad!" said the soldier. "But tell me, old witch, what's in all this for yourself? You can't be doing it for nothing."

"I don't want a single penny," said the witch. "All you need to do for me is collect a dusty old tinderbox that my grandmother forgot when she was last down there."

"Don't let's waste any more time," said the soldier. "Give me the rope; I'll tie it around my middle."

"Here it is," said the witch. "And here's my blue-checked apron."

The soldier climbed up the tree and slid down the hole. *Thump!* He found himself in a great passage, just as the witch had said.

He unlocked the first door. My, my, my! There sat the dog with eyes as big as teacups; it stared and glared at him.

"You're a nice little fellow," said the soldier. He lifted the dog onto the witch's apron and crammed his pockets with coppers. Then he shut the lid, put the dog back on top, and marched into the second room. There sat the dog with eyes as big as millstones.

"You shouldn't stare so hard," said the soldier. "You'll strain your eyes." And he lifted the dog onto the apron. But when he saw the masses of silver coins, he threw away all the coppers and filled his pockets — and knapsack, too — with silver.

Then he went into the third room. This was really frightful! The dog there had eyes as large as the great Round Tower, and they went around and around in its head like wheels.

"Good evening," said the soldier, and he touched his cap politely, for he had never seen a dog like this before. But after he had stared at the creature for a while, he said to himself, "Enough of that!" Then he heaved the dog onto the apron and lifted the lid of the chest. Heavens! What heaps of gold! It was enough to buy the whole of Copenhagen, as well as all the sugar pigs, tin soldiers, whipping tops, and rocking horses in the world. Yes, that was

money all right. Quickly he threw away all the silver coins in his pockets and knapsack and stuffed them with gold instead; then he filled his cap, and after that his boots. Indeed, he could hardly walk! Now for once he really had money. He lifted the dog back on its box, slammed the door behind him, and shouted up the tree, "Hi, old witch! Pull me up again!"

"Have you got the tinderbox?" asked the witch.

"Bless me, old dame, you're right," said the soldier. "It had slipped my mind." And he went back and collected it. The witch hauled him up, and there he stood in the road once more, but now with pockets, cap, knapsack, and boots all bulging out with gold.

"Why do you want the tinderbox?" asked the soldier.

"That's no business of yours," said the witch. "You've got your money; just give me the tinderbox. That was the arrangement."

"Oh, rubbish," said the soldier. "Tell me what you are going to do with it, or I'll cut off your head with my sword."

"No," said the witch. "You're wasting your time."

But she was wrong. The soldier cut off her head, and there she lay. The soldier put all his gold in her apron, tied it into a bundle, and threw it over his shoulder. Then he slipped the tinderbox into his pocket and strode off into the town.

It was a fine town, and the soldier made for the finest inn, where he booked the very best rooms and ordered all his favorite things to eat. He was a rich man now! The servant whose job it was to clean his boots thought, *Funny old boots for such a grand customer* — but the soldier soon put that right. The next day he went out and bought expensive boots and plenty of fine new clothes. He was a proper gentleman now, and people were glad to tell him all about the town, its sights and pleasures, and about the king and the lovely princess, his daughter.

"I wouldn't mind seeing her," said the soldier.

"Not a hope," he was told. "She lives in a big copper castle, with walls and towers all around. No one is allowed to visit except her parents. You see, it has been prophesied that she will marry a common soldier, and the king won't put up with that."

The soldier was now living a merry sort of life. He went to the theater; he drove in his own carriage through the park and gave away handfuls of money to the poor — he hadn't forgotten what it was like to be poor himself. How pleasant it was to be rich and well dressed! Friends flocked around, all telling him what a splendid fellow he was, a real gentleman. He liked that, you may be sure.

But since he was spending money all the time and never earning anything, a day came when he found that he had only two pennies left. He was obliged to leave his grand apartment and move into a poky little attic under the roof. He had not only to clean his own boots, but to mend them, too; he did this with a darning needle. None of his former friends ever called; they didn't want to climb all those stairs.

One evening, when he was sitting in the dark since he couldn't afford a candle, he suddenly remembered that there was a  candle-end in the tinderbox, the one he had brought from the hollow tree. But the moment he struck the flint to make a light, the door flew open, and there before him was the dog with eyes as big as teacups. "What are my lord's commands?" said the dog.

I say, that's an odd sort of tinderbox, thought the soldier. *Can I have whatever I want?* Aloud, he said to the dog, "Bring me some money." *Flick!* It was gone. *Flack!* The dog was back—  with a bag of coppers in its mouth—all in less than a second.

And now the soldier realized what a treasure he possessed. You struck the flint once, he found, for the dog with the copper coins, twice for the dog with silver, and three times for the dog in charge of the gold. So, without much delay, he was back in the grand set of rooms, wearing elegant  clothes. And now, of course, all his friends flocked back; they couldn't get enough of his company.

One day he thought to himself, *It's very odd that no one can see the princess. She's supposed to be such a beauty— but what's the good of that if she has to stay in that copper*

25

castle with all those walls and towers? There must be a way of getting through. Where's my tinderbox? He struck the flint, and — *whoosh!* — there was the dog with eyes as big as teacups.

"I know it's pretty late at night," he said, "but I would like to see that princess, if only for half a minute."

The dog was gone in a flash, and just as quickly returned, with the princess fast asleep on his back. Oh, she was lovely — a real princess, no doubt about that. The soldier couldn't resist giving her a kiss; after all, he was a real soldier. But the half-minute was soon gone, and the dog sped back to the castle with the sleeping girl. In the morning, though, at breakfast with her father and mother, she told them that she had had a very strange dream. A great dog had taken her on a lightning ride, and a soldier had kissed her.

"That's a peculiar story, I must say," said the king.

Now one of the older ladies-in-waiting was told to sit by the princess's bed the next night to see if she had another dream of the same sort — and to see if it *was* a dream. And as it happened, the soldier longed so much for another sight of the princess that on that night he again sent the dog to collect her, and the dog did as he was asked. But the lady-in-waiting was on the alert; she put on her galoshes and followed the dog at a racing speed, and when she saw it vanish with her charge into a big house, she said to herself, "Now we'll know the truth of the matter!" And she chalked a cross on the door. Then she went back to get some sleep.

But the dog was no fool. When it saw a chalked cross on the soldier's door, it took a bit of chalk and put crosses on all the doors in the town. That was clever of him, because now she hadn't a chance of finding the place.

Next morning, the king and queen and a host of court officials were taken by the lady-in-waiting to see the house with the mark.

"Here it is!" said the king, catching sight of a door with a cross.

"No, husband, it's here," said the queen as she looked at another door.

"There's another!" "There's another!" they were all now saying. And soon they realized that it was no use trying to find the right house; they might just as well go home.

But the queen — ah, she was a clever one. She could do more than just ride about in a glittering carriage! She took up her big golden scissors, cut up a piece of silk, and sewed it into a pretty little bag. This she filled with very fine grains of buckwheat. Then she fastened the bag to her daughter's back, snipping a little hole in the silk so that grains would trickle out and mark the path. That night the dog came again, took the princess, and sped with her to the soldier; he was now so much in love that he longed to be a prince and so be able to marry her. But the dog never noticed the trail of grain all the way from the castle to the soldier's window. When morning came, it was plain enough to the king and queen where their daughter had been. They had the soldier seized and put in prison.

There he sat in a dark and wretched cell. And the jailers kept saying to him, "Tomorrow you're to be hanged." He didn't enjoy that at all. The worst of it was, he had left his tinderbox in his room. In the first light of morning, he looked through the iron bars of the little window; there were crowds, all hurrying past to see him hanged. Drums were sounding for the event; soldiers were marching briskly. Everyone was rushing to get a good view. Quite near, he saw a cobbler's boy in a leather apron and slippers; he was scurrying along so fast that one of his slippers flew off and struck the wall near where the soldier was peering out from behind the bars.

"I say, cobbler's boy," said the soldier. "You don't have to hurry; they can't begin without me. Wait, though — if you run along to my place and fetch my tinderbox, you'll have sixpence for yourself. But you'll have to be quick!"

The boy was only too glad to earn a coin or two, and raced off. He was

soon back with the tinderbox, gave it to the soldier, and—well, listen carefully and you'll know what happened.

Outside the town, a gallows had been built. Around it stood the soldiers, and crowded behind were thousands and thousands of people. The king and queen sat on a splendid throne; the judges and councilors sat directly opposite. As for the soldier, he had already climbed the ladder to the platform, but just as they were going to put the rope around his neck, and there was a moment's silence, he called out, "Don't forget the custom: Anyone about to be hanged is allowed a last small request, and mine's a little one. I just want to smoke a pipe of tobacco, my last in this world."

The king couldn't very well say no to that, so the soldier took out the tinderbox to strike a light. *One! Two! Three!* he struck. And there stood all three dogs: the one with eyes as big as teacups, the one with eyes like millstones, and the third with eyes as huge as the Round Tower.

"Now, you three, save me from being hanged!" said the soldier. At once the dogs leaped upon the judges and councilors, seizing some by the legs and some by the nose, and tossed them into the air. When they came down, they were dashed to pieces.

"Not me—I won't be tossed!" cried the king. But the biggest dog picked up both king and queen and sent them hurtling into the air like the others. The guards and soldiers were terrified, but the people were delighted with the fun. They called out, "Little soldier, you be our king and marry the princess!" They lifted the soldier into the royal carriage, and the three dogs frisked about in front, barking in their own way, "Hurrah! Hurrah!" The urchins and young apprentices whistled through their fingers; the guards presented arms. The princess stepped down from her copper castle and became the queen. She liked that, I can tell you. The wedding feast lasted a whole week, while the three dogs sat at the table and rolled their eyes at all the other guests.

Thumbelina

*T*his tale was written and published in 1835, the same year as Andersen's first trial booklet. "Thumbelina" appeared in a second booklet in good time for Christmas. To write of a tiny fairy-tale human was no problem to Andersen, a master of doll-sized toy theater all his life. As a writer, the small scale was always to serve him well. The "Tom Thumb" of the Grimms and the wild fantasies of E. T. A. Hoffmann (remembered now only for the ballet themes of The Nutcracker *and* Coppélia*)* would have been known to Andersen, but his version of the tiny odyssey was entirely his own. Not only the manner of telling but also the features within make "Thumbelina" a real Andersen original. The details at once divide him from the traditional pattern, not only by such items as the walnut-shell bed, the soup-plate pond, and such, but also by, for example, the awesome moment when life returns to the bird. Again, as in so many later tales, how intrinsic to the event is the changing landscape through the changing seasons — the wintry stubble field, for instance, perceived as a forest. Memorable, too, are the characters — the field mouse and mole in particular. (Did Kenneth Grahame know this tale? He must have. But he was a good deal kinder to Mole and Rat and the rest — even to Toad.)

And there is the author himself, an approving listener at the end. The "warm countries" mark his discovery of and lasting love for Italy and the south. A friendly adult critic might also praise how cunningly the points of sadness and grief are lightened by secret humor and open joy at the (well-earned) turns of luck and surprise in the journey.

ONCE UPON A TIME THERE WAS a woman who wanted a little tiny child of her own, but she didn't know how to set about finding one. So off she went to an old witch and said to her, "I would so much like to have a little child! Couldn't you tell me where to get one?"

"Oh, that's not difficult," said the witch. "Here's a barleycorn for you—and it isn't the kind that grows in the farmer's field, nor the kind that the chickens eat, either. Just put it in a flowerpot, and you shall see what you shall see!"

"Oh, thank you!" said the woman, and she gave the witch a silver coin. Then she went home and planted the grain. She hadn't long to wait before a fine big flower sprang up; it looked like a tulip, but the petals were tightly closed, as if it were still a bud.

"What a lovely flower!" said the woman, and she kissed the closed red-and-yellow petals. The moment she did so, the flower burst open with a loud crack. It was a real tulip—you could see that now—but right in the middle of the flower, on the green center, sat a tiny little girl, as graceful and delicate as a fairy. She was no more than a thumb-joint high, and so she was called Thumbelina.

She was given a walnut shell, beautifully polished, as her bed; she lay on a mattress of deep-blue violet petals, and a rose petal was her eiderdown. There she slept at night, but in the daytime she played upon the table, where the woman had put a soup plate of water with a circle of flowers around its edge, the stalks facing the center. Floating in the plate was a large tulip petal, on which Thumbelina could sit and row from one side to the other, using two white horsehairs as oars. It was the prettiest sight! She could sing, too, in the tiniest, sweetest voice ever heard.

One night, as she lay in her beautiful bed, a toad came hopping into the room, through a broken windowpane. The toad looked very big and wet as she thumped down onto the table where Thumbelina lay fast asleep under her rose petal.

"Now *there* be a handsome wife for my son!" said the toad. And she took the walnut-shell bed in which the little girl was sleeping and hopped with it through the window and down into the garden. At the end of the garden flowed a wide stream, but at the edge, it was marshy and thick with mud; this was where the toad lived with her son. He was not at all handsome; in fact, he looked just like his mother. "Croak, croak! Brek-kek-kex!" That was all he would say when he saw the pretty little girl in the walnut shell.

"Don't speak so loudly, or she'll wake," said the old toad. "She could still escape from us, for she's as light as a piece of swan's down. I know — we'll put her out in the stream on one of the great water-lily leaves; she will think it an island, for she is such a tiny wisp of a creature. While she is there, we can start preparing the best room under the mud, where you two will make your home together."

Out in the stream grew a great many water lilies, with wide green leaves that looked as if they were floating free on the water. The leaf that lay farthest out was also the biggest of all, and that was where the old toad set down the walnut shell with Thumbelina inside. The poor little creature woke up very early the next morning, and when she saw where she was, she began to cry bitterly, for there was water all around the big leaf, and no possible way of getting back to land.

Meanwhile, the old toad stayed down below in the mud, busily decorating the room with rushes and yellow water-flowers to make it look nice and bright for her new daughter-in-law. Then she swam out again, this time taking her son, to the leaf where Thumbelina was waiting. They had come to fetch the pretty walnut-shell bed so that they could put it in the bridal bedroom before the little bride arrived. The old toad, while still in the water, made a deep bow to Thumbelina and said, "This is my son; he is going to be your husband, and the pair of you will live very happily in a fine home down in the mud."

"Croak, croak! Brek-kek-kex!" was all that the son could say.

Then they took the elegant little bed and swam off with it, while Thumbelina sat all alone on the green leaf crying, for she had no wish to live with the old toad or to have her son for a husband. Now, the little fish, swimming below in the water, had seen the toad and had heard what she said, so they thrust their heads up to see the little girl for themselves. As soon as they did so, they realized how lovely she was, and it grieved them to think that she had to go and live in the mud with the toad.

No, that must never happen! So they gathered together in the water around the green stalk of the leaf that she was on, and gnawed and gnawed it through.

Off went the leaf, floating along the stream, carrying Thumbelina far, far away, where the toads could not follow.

On and on she sailed, and the birds in the trees sang out, "What a pretty little creature!" as they caught sight of her.

Farther and farther along glided the leaf—and that was how Thumbelina journeyed into another country.

A lovely white butterfly fluttered around her, and at last it alighted on the leaf, for it had taken a fancy to the little girl. How happy she was now! The toads could no longer reach her, and everything was beautiful, wherever she looked. The water, where the sun shone, was just like gleaming gold. Thumbelina took her sash, gave one end to the friendly butterfly, and tied the other to the leaf; now she sped along even more swiftly.

Just then, a big cockchafer beetle came flying by; he saw the little girl, and in a flash he grasped her slender waist in his claws and flew up with her into a tree. The green leaf went floating on down the stream, taking the butterfly with it.

Goodness! How frightened poor Thumbelina was when the cockchafer carried her off! And she grieved, too, for her friend the white butterfly. But the beetle cared nothing about that. He alighted on the largest green leaf of the tree and set her down, then gave her honeydew from the flowers to eat, and told her that she was very pretty (though not in the least like a cockchafer).

Presently all the other cockchafers who lived in the tree came to call on her. They looked at her, and the young lady cockchafers shrugged their feelers and said, "But she has only two legs, the miserable little insect!" and "She hasn't any feelers!" and "Her waist is so thin—ugh! She looks quite like a human! How ugly she is!" That was the sort of thing they went on saying—and yet Thumbelina was really the prettiest little creature.

The cockchafer who had carried her off thought this, certainly, but when all the other beetles declared that she was a fright to look at, he too began to think her ugly and at last would have nothing more to do with her; she could go wherever she chose. Several beetles flew down from the tree with her and put her on a daisy; there she sat and wept because she was so ugly that the cockchafers would have nothing to do with her—and yet she was the most beautiful little thing you could imagine, lovelier than the most perfect of rose petals.

All through the summer, poor Thumbelina lived quite alone in the great forest. She wove herself a bed out of blades of grass and hung it like a hammock under a large sorrel leaf as shelter from the rain. For her food she gathered honey and pollen from flowers, and she drank the dew that lay every morning on the leaves. So the summer and autumn passed but then came winter, the long, cold winter. The birds that had sung so delightfully now flew far away; the trees lost their leaves; the flowers withered. Then the big sorrel leaf, which had been her roof, curled up and shriveled, until nothing was left of it but a dry yellow stalk. Thumbelina was terribly cold, for her clothes were all in rags and she was so fragile and small. It seemed that she would soon be frozen to death. The snow began to fall, and every snowflake that fell on her was as heavy as a shovelful thrown on one of us. After all, she was only an inch high. So she wrapped herself in a withered leaf, but that did not warm her, and she shivered more and more.

By this time she had wandered to the edge of the forest. Just outside lay a large cornfield, but the corn had long been gathered and now only the bare dry stubble stood up out of the frozen ground. For her this was like a forest to travel through, and — oh, oh, oh! — how she shook with the cold. Then she came to a field mouse's door, which led to a little house under the stubble. There the field mouse lived, snug and comfortable, with a store-room full of corn, a warm kitchen, and a dining room. Poor Thumbelina stood at the door like any little beggar girl and asked if she might have a piece of barley seed, for she had had nothing at all to eat for the past two days.

"You poor little thing!" said the field mouse, for she was a kind old creature at heart. "Come into my warm kitchen and have something to eat with me." She enjoyed Thumbelina's company, so presently she said, "You are welcome to stay with me for the winter, only you must keep my place nice and clean, and tell me stories; I am very fond of stories." Thumbelina did what the good old field mouse asked, and the time passed happily enough.

"We shall soon be having a visitor," said the field mouse. "My neighbor comes to visit me every week. His house is even better than mine; he has such fine large rooms, and he wears such a handsome black velvet coat! If you could only get him for a husband, you would be well provided for. But his sight isn't good. You must be ready to tell the best stories you know."

Thumbelina did not like the thought of this. She had no wish to marry the wealthy neighbor, the mole, who was coming to call in his black velvet coat. The field mouse reminded Thumbelina how rich and learned he was; she told her that his house was twenty times as big as the one that they were in, that he knew about many things, though he did not care for the sun and the beautiful flowers, for he had never seen them. Thumbelina had to sing for him, and she sang "I Had a Little Nut Tree," and "Ladybug, Ladybug, Fly Away Home." The mole fell in love with her because of her sweet voice, but he kept this to himself, for he was a very cautious man.

He had recently dug himself a long passage through the earth, linking his own house to theirs, and he gave the field mouse and Thumbelina permission to walk through whenever they wished. But he begged them not to be afraid of the bird that lay in the passage. He told them that the bird was quite unmarked and uninjured, with all its feathers and beak; it must have died quite recently, with the coming of winter, and had somehow fallen into his underground path.

Then the mole took in his mouth a piece of rotten wood (for that glows just like a fire in the dark) and went ahead to light the long, dark passage for his guests. Soon they came to the place where the bird was lying, and the mole thrust his broad nose up against the roof and pushed through the earth so that there was a hole to let in the daylight. And there could be seen a swallow with its beautiful wings pressed close against its sides, its legs and head huddled into its feathers; the poor bird must surely have died of cold. Thumbelina felt sorry for it; she loved all the little birds that had sung and twittered to her so delightfully all the summer long. But the mole pushed the swallow aside with his short legs, and said, "There's one that we shan't hear whistling anymore! What a fate to be born a little bird! Thank heaven none of my children will ever be one. A bird can do nothing but say *tweet-tweet* and then starve to death in the winter."

"Yes, you have a point there," said the field mouse. "What has a bird to show for all its *tweet-tweet-tweet* when winter comes? It starves and freezes. And yet everyone thinks so highly of them."

Thumbelina said not a word, but when the others had moved on, she

bent down, gently parted the feathers on its head, and kissed its closed eyes. *Perhaps*, she thought, *this is the one that sang to me so sweetly during the summer. What happiness it gave me, that dear little woodland bird!*

Then the mole stopped up the daylight hole in the roof and escorted the ladies home.

But that night Thumbelina could not sleep at all, so she got out of bed and wove a coverlet of hay; this done, she carried it along and spread it

over the bird. At its side she laid some soft thistledown that she had found in the field mouse's living room, so that it might rest warm in the cold earth. "Farewell, you pretty little bird," she said. "Farewell, and thank you for your lovely song in the summer, when the trees were green and the sun shone so joyfully on us all." And then she laid her head on the bird's heart — but at once she felt greatly startled, for it seemed as if

something was knocking inside. It was the bird's heart, beating. He was not dead; he was only numb with cold, and now that he had been warmed, he began to revive.

In autumn the swallows all fly away to warmer lands. But if one of them is delayed, the cold can freeze its life away; it falls to the ground and is soon buried under the snow.

Thumbelina trembled with shock; the bird was so much larger than herself, for she was only an inch high. But she gathered her courage and tucked the thistledown closer around the poor bird, and then ran back for her own bedcover, a mint leaf, to place over his head.

The next night she crept out again to visit him — and now he was certainly alive, but so weak that he could open his eyes for only a moment

to look at Thumbelina. There she stood with a piece of rotten wood in her hand, for she had no other lantern.

"Thank you, thank you, pretty little girl," said the sick swallow. "You have warmed me so well that I shall soon be strong again, and fly in the bright sunshine."

"Oh," said Thumbelina, "it is still cold outside — snow and frost everywhere. Stay in your warm bed meanwhile, and I shall take care of you."

Then she brought the swallow some water in a leaf, and the bird drank, and told her how he had injured one of his wings on a thornbush and so had not been able to fly as fast as the other swallows when they had journeyed to warmer lands. At last he had fallen to the ground, and remembered no more; he could not imagine how he had come to be where he was lying now.

All through the winter, the swallow remained in the passage. Thumbelina looked after him and grew very fond of him. But she said nothing of this to the mole or the field mouse, for they did not care for birds. At length, the spring came and the sun's rays began to pierce through the earth. The swallow said goodbye to Thumbelina and reopened the hole that the mole had made in the roof of the passage. The sunshine filled them both with joy, and the swallow asked Thumbelina to come away with him; she could sit on his back, and they would fly far off into the leafy green wood. But Thumbelina knew that the old field mouse would be upset if she left like that.

"No, I cannot come," she said.

"Then farewell, farewell, you kind, pretty girl," said the swallow, and he flew out into the sunshine. Thumbelina watched him soar into the sky, and her eyes filled with tears, for she had become very fond of the poor swallow.

"*Tweet, tweet!*" sang the bird, and flew off into the leafy wood.

Thumbelina was now very sad. She was not allowed to go out into the bright daylight, and in the field where they lived, the corn grew so tall that for her it was like a forest towering overhead.

"You must get your trousseau ready this summer," said the field mouse, for their neighbor, the mole with the velvet coat, had made Thumbelina an offer of marriage. "You must have clothes both of linen and wool, and plenty of blankets and sheets, when you are the wife of the mole."

Thumbelina had to work hard with her spindle, and the mole hired four spiders to weave for her, night and day. Every evening he would pay  them a visit, and every time he would say that when the summer was over, and the sun was not so dreadfully hot and had stopped baking the earth as hard as a stone, then they would have the wedding. But Thumbelina was not at all happy, for she did not care for the pompous old mole. Every morning when the sun rose, and every evening when it set, she would creep outside; when the wind blew the ears of corn apart, she could see the blue sky, and she thought each time how beautiful and bright it was in the open air. She wished so much to see her dear swallow again, but he did not come back; he had flown away into the green and leafy wood.

When autumn came, the whole of Thumbelina's trousseau was ready. "In four weeks' time," said the field mouse, "you shall have your wedding." But Thumbelina wept and said that she did not want to marry the mole.

"Nonsense!" said the field mouse. "Don't be so difficult. You are getting a splendid husband. Why, the queen herself has not such a fine black velvet coat. And think of his well-stocked kitchen and cellar! Be thankful for your good fortune."

And so the wedding day arrived. The mole had already come to fetch Thumbelina; she was to go and live with him deep under the earth; she would never be able to go up into the radiant sunshine, for the mole could not stand the light. Full of grief, she went to say a last goodbye to the glorious sun — she had always at least been allowed to come to the doorway while she was living with the field mouse.

"Farewell, bright sun!" she said, holding up her arms toward it, and she walked a few steps into the open world. The corn had been harvested and now only the stubble was left. "Farewell, farewell," she said again, and she threw her arms around a little red flower still growing among the stalks. "If ever you see the swallow again, tell him I send my love."

At that very moment she heard a sound — *Tweet, tweet!* — exactly overhead. It was the swallow. How glad he was to see his Thumbelina! And then she told him that on this day she had to marry the mole and go to live in a dark house under the earth, where the sun never shone. And the tears rained from her eyes at the thought of it.

"The cold winter is coming on," said the swallow. "I am flying far away to the warm countries. Won't you come with me? You can sit on my back and tie yourself on with your sash; then we shall leave the mole and his dark house and fly far, far away over the mountains to a land where the sun shines even more beautifully than here, where it is always summer and the groves and trees are full of the loveliest flowers. Ah, come with me, dear little Thumbelina, you who saved my life when I lay frozen in the dark passage under the earth."

"Yes, I will go with you," said Thumbelina. She seated herself on the bird's back and tied her sash to one of his strongest feathers. And then the swallow soared high up into the air, over forest and lake, over great mountains where the snow always lies. The frosty air made Thumbelina shiver, but she crept under the bird's warm feathers and just peeped out to gaze at the wonderful scenes below.

At last they came to the warm countries. There the sun shone much more brilliantly than Thumbelina had ever known it. The sky seemed twice as high, and along the roadside hedges grew the most delicious green and purple grapes. Lemons and oranges hung from trees, the air was fragrant with myrtle and many sweet herbs, and about the paths ran many lovely children, playing among the brightly colored butterflies. But the swallow flew farther and farther still, where the scene grew more and more beautiful. And there, under great green trees, by a lake of sapphire blue, stood a palace, built long ago of dazzling white marble, with vines growing around its tall pillars. Right on top of the pillars were many swallows' nests, and in one of them lived Thumbelina's bird.

"Here is my home," he said. "But if you would like to choose for yourself one of these beautiful flowers growing just below, I will set you down on it, and you shall live there as happily as you could wish."

"Ah, how I should love that!" she cried, clapping her little hands.

A great white column lay fallen on the ground. It had broken into three pieces, and between them grew beautiful tall white flowers. The swallow flew down with Thumbelina and set her on one of the petals. And what a surprise she had! There, in the middle of the flower, was a little prince, as fine and delicate as if he were made of glass. He had the prettiest gold crown upon his head and bright and shining wings upon his shoulders, and he was no bigger than Thumbelina herself.

He was the guardian spirit of the flower. In every flower was a little creature just like himself, but this one was king of them all.

"How beautiful he is!" whispered Thumbelina to the swallow. The little prince was at first quite alarmed at the bird, who seemed a giant to him, but when he beheld Thumbelina, he was filled with joy — he thought her the loveliest girl he had ever seen, even among his flower fairies. He took his golden crown from his head and laid it on hers, and asked what her name was and if she would consent to be his wife and queen of all the flowers.

Well, this was a husband she could truly love — very different from the toad's son or the old mole with his velvet coat. And so she said yes to the handsome prince. Then from every flower rose a tiny creature, girl or boy, man or lady, so small and so beautiful that it was thrilling to see them. Each one brought Thumbelina a present, but best of all was a pair of beautiful wings. They were fastened to Thumbelina's shoulders, and now she too could fly from flower to flower. Everyone rejoiced; it was like a wonderful summer party. The swallow in his nest above joined in and sang for them the finest song he knew. But he was sad at heart, for he was so fond of Thumbelina that he never wished to be parted from her.

"You shall not be called Thumbelina anymore," said the flower prince. "It is not pretty enough for one as beautiful as you. We shall call you Maia."

"Goodbye, goodbye," said the swallow when it was time once again for him to fly away from the warm countries to Denmark. There he had a little nest by the window of the man who tells fairy tales. "Listen, listen," the swallow trilled to the fairy-tale teller — and that is how we come to know this story.

45

This is a funny tale — there's no doubt about that — with a particularly saucy ending. An early work (1837), it has still lost none of its edge. It is popular with the young, but it also has something serious to say for everybody.

Late in his life, Andersen was shown the design for a statue of himself, reading aloud to unseen listeners but with children clambering over him. "I write for everyone," he said (I summarize his words). "The comic part is enjoyed by children, but there are more and more levels within each tale, as everyone who reads the tales again will discover. And," he added, "I do not read to listeners around my head or on my knee." The statue may be seen today in a Copenhagen park — without the clambering young. You yourself, passerby (child or adult), are the listener.

Still, you need not be young, nor old, to find out what Andersen meant in this teasing tale. If people continue to do something stupid or cruel because "everyone does it" or because "it's an old tradition, so it must be all right" — well, as we can see all through history, that's where trouble lies. This is as true today and tomorrow as it was yesterday.

Only one voice spoke the truth in Andersen's story — and that was the voice of a child, still too young to have met with peer pressure. Yet here is a strange fact: The original tale had a different ending, but Andersen felt dissatisfied. Suddenly the answer came to him. He rushed to the printer, seized the manuscript, and supplied the ending — and the child — we know.

Now write down all the bad or stupid things that come to your mind — things that too many people accept against their common sense, as everyone did the emperor's new clothes.

ANY YEARS AGO THERE WAS AN EMPEROR who loved fine clothes more than anything else in the world. Indeed, dressing up took all his time. Did he care to inspect his army? Or go to the theater? Or ride out in his carriage among the people? Not at all—except as a chance to show off his latest splendid clothes. He had a different coat for every hour of the day. At the times when you would be told of other monarchs, "He is in council," this emperor (if you asked) would be "in his dressing room."

Life was cheerful anyway in the city. Strangers were always arriving, and one day a pair of shady characters turned up. Well, that's what they were, but they called themselves weavers. What's more, they declared that the cloth they wove was not only of marvelous beauty but also had magical

properties: whether on the loom or made into clothes, it was invisible to anyone who was unfit for his job or particularly stupid. *Excellent!* thought the emperor. *Here's a real chance to find out which of my people aren't fit for the posts they hold—and I can sort out the wise from the fools. Yes! That stuff must be woven and made into clothes at once.* And he gave the weavers a large sum of money so that they could start.

Right away the rascally pair set up their looms and behaved as if they were working hard. But actually there was nothing on the looms at all. Soon the men were demanding the finest silk and golden thread; these they crammed into their own pockets, and then they just went on moving their arms, as if they were weaving, far into the night.

After a time, the emperor thought, *I really would like to know how they are getting on.*

But when he remembered that the cloth could not be seen by anyone who was stupid or unfit for his work, he felt rather awkward about going himself. Of course he had no doubts about his own abilities — still, it might be a good idea to send someone else. After all, everyone in the city had heard by now about the special powers of the cloth; everyone was longing to find out how stupid or incompetent his neighbors were.

I know what I'll do, thought the emperor. *I'll send my honest old chief minister. He's the right man, as sensible as can be, and no one can complain about his work. Yes, that's the answer.*

So the good old minister went along to the room where the false weavers were making a busy show of working at the looms. *Heaven help us!* thought the old man. *I can't see any cloth.*

However wide he opened his eyes, there was nothing. But he kept this to himself.

Then the two cheats begged him to step closer.

"Look at the patterns, noble sir. Aren't they beautiful? And the colors—have you ever seen any like these?" And they waved their hands at the empty looms.

The poor minister peered and stared, but he still could see nothing. The reason was simple; nothing was there to see.

Heavens above! he thought. *Am I really stupid after all? That has never occurred to me, and it had better not occur to anyone else. Am I really unfit to be minister? No—no—it would never do to say that I can't see the cloth.*

"Well, don't you admire it?" said one of the tricksters, still moving his hands. "You haven't said a word."

"Oh, it's charming, charming, quite delightful," said the poor old man, peering through his spectacles. "The patterns—the colors—yes, I must tell the emperor that they seem to me quite remarkable."

"That's very encouraging," said the tricksters, and they pointed out more and more details of the cloth's design. The old man listened carefully so that he could repeat it all to the emperor. And this he did.

Soon the rogues were demanding a further supply of money, silk, and golden thread. They had to have it, they declared, to finish the cloth. But again, whatever they were given was promptly stuffed into their own deep pockets. Of course not a stitch of cloth appeared, though the cheats went on busily moving their hands at the empty looms.

Presently the emperor decided to send another honest official to see how the weaving was going on. "Ask how soon the stuff will be ready," the worthy man was told. But the same thing happened to him as to the minister. He looked and looked, but since there was nothing to see but empty looms, nothing was all he saw.

"Isn't it lovely?" said one the of the rascals, and they lifted up the imaginary cloth and held it before the visitor. "See the designs, the colors." And they pointed out the beauties that did not exist.

I don't believe I'm stupid, thought the official. *But maybe I'm not good enough at my work. Well, that has never before been questioned, and it had better not be questioned now.* So he made admiring noises about the cloth he could not see. "Yes, yes, very handsome — splendid colors — superb design." And he reported to the emperor that the weaving was "magnificent!"

The news of the wonderful fabric soon ran through the city. At last the emperor made up his mind to look at it for himself. So, with the two who had already been and a carefully chosen group of court attendants, he went to the weaving room. There were the two cheats in front of the empty looms acting as busy as ever.

The two who had been before were the first to speak. "What splendid cloth!" said the old minister. And the other official murmured praise about the pattern and the colors.

As they spoke, they pointed to the empty looms; they were sure that everyone else could see the lengths of stuff.

This is terrible! thought the emperor. *I can't see a thing on the looms! Am I stupid? Am I unfit to be emperor? What a frightful notion! I mustn't let myself think of it—nor must anyone else.* He then said aloud, "Such charming material, charming! It has our highest approval." And he nodded in a satisfied way toward the empty looms. No one must guess that he saw nothing there at all.

The courtiers stared hard too, but not one of them saw a single thread of cloth. No wonder each of them secretly felt alarm. But aloud they echoed the emperor's words. "Charming!" "Charming!" They even advised the emperor to use the material for a new set of robes to wear in the great procession that would soon be taking place. "It is magnificent—so unusual!" Every courtier

felt obliged to murmur something of the kind. And the emperor gave each of the swindlers an honorable decoration and the title of Imperial Court Official of the Loom.

On the eve of the great procession, the cheats were still at work on their imaginary task—the making of clothes. All through the night they busied themselves by the light of at least sixteen candles. The outfit had to be finished in time. To the waiting courtiers, the weavers seemed to be taking heavy folds of stuff from the loom; they seemed to be cutting, with big tailor's scissors, at something invisible;

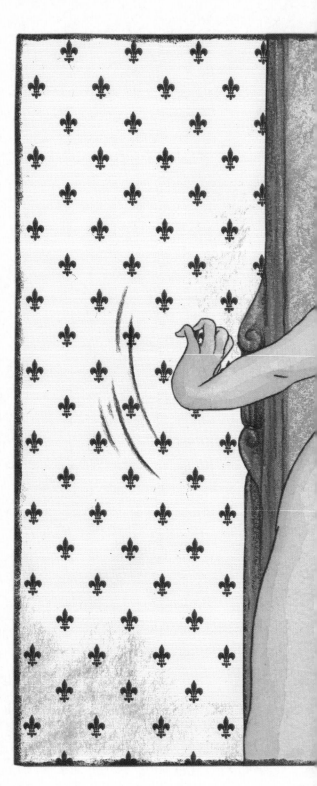

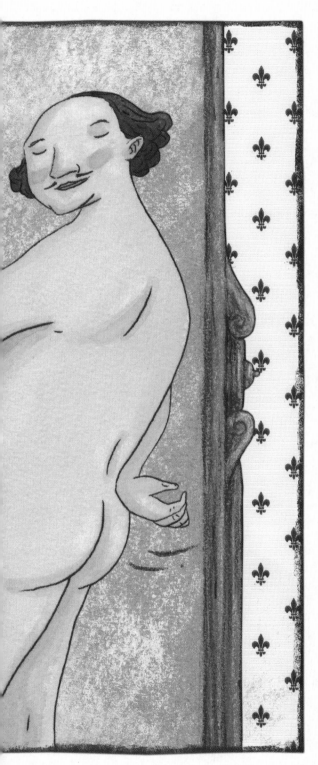

they seemed to be stitching away with needles that had no thread. At last they announced: "The clothes are ready!"

And now the emperor made his way to the room with the most noble of his courtiers. At once the tricksters held up their arms as if they were lifting something. "Here is the jacket, your Imperial Highness. Here is the cloak." And so they went on. "Their special quality is that they are as light as gossamer. You might think from the feel that you were wearing nothing at all — but that makes them differ from all the usual heavy and cumbersome robes."

"Yes, indeed," said all the courtiers. But since there was nothing there to see, nothing was all they saw.

The rogues went on. "If your Imperial Highness will graciously take off the clothes he is wearing now, we shall have the honor of putting on the new ones here; you can see the effect yourself in the great mirror."

So the emperor took off his clothes, and the impudent pair pretended to hand him the new set, one thing at a time. Finally they made a show of fastening on his train. The imaginary costume was complete.

The emperor turned and twisted about in front of the glass. "How elegant it looks!" "What a perfect fit!" murmured the courtiers. "What rich material!" "Such splendid colors!" "Have you ever seen more magnificent robes?" No one would dare to admit that he saw nothing.

"Your Imperial Highness," said the Chief Master of Ceremonies, "the canopy waits outside." The canopy was to be carried over his head in the procession.

"Well," said the emperor, "I am ready. I agree with you that it is really an excellent fit." Once again he turned this way and that, for his final look at the mirror. The courtiers who were to carry the train bent down as if to lift something from the floor. *They* were not going to let people think that they saw nothing there.

So the emperor walked forth in stately procession under the splendid canopy. People in the streets or at the windows called out such things as

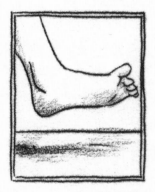

"Doesn't he look magnificent!," "Those new clothes! Aren't they marvelous!," and "What elegance!" Can you imagine! Nobody dared admit that he or she couldn't see any clothes at all. That would have meant that the person was a stupid fool, or no good at his job. Indeed, not one of the emperor's gorgeous outfits had ever been so much praised.

Then, in a moment's silence, a child's puzzled voice was heard. "He's got nothing on!"

"Shh!" said the child's father. "These little ones do talk nonsense."

But a whisper moved through the crowd. "A child over there says that the emperor has nothing on!" "The emperor has nothing on!"

At last the emperor himself began to think that they could be right. But then he thought, *If I stop, it will spoil the procession. And that would never do.*

So on he stepped, even more proudly than before. As for the courtiers, they went on carrying a train that was not there at all. ⌒

First published in 1837, this powerful tale made such an impact on critics and readers that Andersen cast off all doubts about his new path as a writer. Its success isn't hard to understand. With its striking and disturbing plot and the spell of the writing — not least in the marvelous opening and, throughout, the pervading sense of the sea, in calm, in storm, in the unknown ocean depths — how could it fail? Even that core of horror, the hideous sea witch in her lair, stays within the enchantment.

And yet — all the beauty and drama apart — to thinking readers today, this is a troubling tale. What is the nature of this "soul," whose owning and acquiring have so little to do with merit or piety? Why did the mermaid really desire a soul? Are the cruelties overplayed, especially when Andersen knows that they'll fail to achieve their aim? The selective allotment of souls raises uneasy questions. Are all beings eligible?

The curious ending to the tale was no consoling afterthought, either for the reader or for the girl herself. The usual myth-supplied route to soul-gaining (winning a human's love) did not satisfy Andersen; he offered a more "divine" way — three hundred years of toilsome good deeds. This was his own invention and his pride. An odd fact is that various people who read the tale as children, though vague now over detail, strangely remember it with love. Not one of them seems to recall the worthy close. (No matter. The mermaid tale remains the national myth of Denmark, with the winsome statue as reminder.)

AR, FAR OUT TO SEA, the water is as blue as the petals of the loveliest cornflower and as clear as the clearest glass; but it is deep, very deep, deeper than any anchor has ever sunk. Countless church towers would have to be placed one on top of another to reach from the seabed to the surface. Down in those depths live the mer-people.

Now, you must not think for a moment that there is nothing down below but bare white sand. No, indeed—the most wonderful trees and plants grow there, with stems and leaves so lithe and sensitive that they wave and sway with the slightest stir of the water; they might be living creatures. All kinds of fish, both large and small, glide in and out of the branches, just like birds in the air up here. In the very deepest part of all is the mer-king's palace. Its walls are of coral, and the long, pointed windows are of the clearest amber, while the roof is made of cockleshells, which open and close with the waves. That's a splendid sight, for each holds a shining pearl; any single one would be the pride of a queen's crown.

The mer-king here had been a widower for many years, and his dowager mother kept house for him. She was a wise old lady, though rather too proud of her royal rank; that's why she always wore twelve oysters on her tail while other highborn mer-folk were allowed no more than six.

But she deserved special praise for the care she took of the little mer-princesses, her granddaughters.

There were six of them, all beautiful, and the youngest was the most beautiful of all. Her skin was like a rose petal, pure and clear; her eyes were as blue as the deepest lake. But, like the others, she had no feet; her body ended in a fish's tail. All day long she and her sisters would play down there in the palace, in and out of the vast rooms where living sea flowers grew from the walls. When the great amber windows were open, the fish would swim inside and let themselves be stroked.

Outside the palace was a large garden with flame-red and sea-blue trees. The fruit shone like gold, and the flowers looked like glowing fire among the moving stems and leaves. The ground itself was of the finest sand, but blue as a sulfur flame. A strange blue-violet light lay over everything; you might have thought that, instead of being far down under the sea, you were high up in the air, with nothing over or under you but sky. On days of perfect calm you could see the sun; it looked like a crimson flower, with rays of light streaming out of its center.

Each of the little princesses had her own small plot in the garden, where she could dig and plant whatever she wished. One made her flower bed in the shape of a whale; another made hers like a mermaid. But the youngest had hers perfectly round, like the sun, and the only flowers she planted there were like smaller suns in their glow and color.

She was a strange child, quiet and thoughtful. While the other sisters decorated their gardens with wonderful things from the wrecks of ships, the only ornament she would have was a beautiful marble carving, a lovely boy made out of pure white stone. This, too, had sunk to the seabed from a wreck.

Beside this marble boy she planted a rose-red tree like a weeping willow, which grew apace, its branches bending over the stone figure until they touched the deep-blue sand below.

Nothing pleased the youngest princess more than to hear about the far-off world of humans. She made the old grandmother tell her all she knew about ships and towns, people and animals. It was a strange and wonderful thought to her that the flowers on earth had a sweet smell, for they had none at all in the sea.

"As soon as you are fifteen," the grandmother told her granddaughters, "you may rise to the surface and sit on the rocks in the moonlight and watch the great ships sail by. If you have enough courage, you may even see woods and towns!" The following year the oldest of the sisters would be fifteen, but as for the others — well, each was a year younger than the next, so the youngest of them all still had six years to wait. But each promised to tell the rest what she had seen and what she had found most surprising in the human world above. Their grandmother never told them enough, and there was so much they wanted to know.

But none of the six had a greater wish to learn about the mysterious earth above than the youngest (the very one who had the longest time to wait), the one who was so thoughtful and quiet. Many a night she would stand at the open window and gaze up through the dark-blue water where the fish frisked with waving fins and tails. She could see the moon and stars; their light was rather pale, to be sure, but seen through the water, they looked much larger than they do to us. If ever a kind of dark cloud glided along beneath them, she knew that it was either a whale swimming over her or a ship full of human people. Those humans never imagined that a beautiful little mermaid was below, stretching up her white hands toward the keel.

And now came the time when the eldest princess turned fifteen and was allowed to rise to the surface. As soon as she was home again, she had a hundred things to tell the others. But what did she like best of all? Lying on a sandbank in the moonlight when the sea was calm, she told them, gazing at the big city, near the coast, where the lights were twinkling like a hundred stars; listening to the busy noise and stir of traffic and people, seeing all the towers and spires of the churches, hearing the ringing of the bells. And just because she couldn't go to the city, she longed to do this more than anything.

Oh, how intently the youngest sister listened! And later in the evening, when she stood at the open window and gazed up through the dark-blue water, she thought of the great city, and then she seemed to hear the ring of church bells echoing all the way down to her.

The next year the second sister was allowed to rise up through the water and swim wherever she wished. She reached the surface just as the sun was going down, and that was the sight that she thought loveliest of all. The whole sky was a blaze of gold, she said; as for the clouds — well, she couldn't find words to describe how beautiful they were, crimson and violet, sailing high overhead. But moving much more swiftly, a flock of wild swans like a long, white ribbon had flown across the waves toward the setting sun. She, too, had swum toward the sun, but it sank in the water, and the brightness vanished from sea and sky.

The year after that, the third sister had her chance. She was the most adventurous so far, and swam up a wide river that flowed into the sea. She saw green hills planted with grapevines; she had glimpses of farms and castles through the trees of the great forests. She heard the singing of birds, and she felt the warmth of the sun — indeed, it was so hot that she often had to dive down to cool her burning

61

face. In the curve of a little bay, a group of human children splashed about in the water, quite naked; she wanted to play with them, but they scampered off in fright.

The fourth sister was not so bold. She kept to midocean, well away from the shore, and that, she declared, gave the best view of all; you could see for miles around. She had seen ships, but so far away that they looked like seagulls. The friendly dolphins had turned somersaults; great whales had spouted jets of water — it was like being surrounded by a hundred waterfalls.

Then came the turn of the fifth sister. Her birthday happened to fall in winter, and so she saw what the others had not seen on their first view of the world above. The sea looked quite green; great icebergs floated about, each one as beautiful as a pearl, she said — yet vaster than the church towers built by men. They appeared in the strangest shapes, glittering like diamonds. She had seated herself on one of the largest, and the sailors in passing ships had been filled with terror, and steered in wide curves as far away as they could get from the iceberg where she sat, her long hair streaming in the wind. Late that evening, the sky had become heavy and overcast; lightning flashed, thunder rolled and rumbled, and the dark waves lifted huge blocks of ice high into the air. Sails were lowered on all the ships; humans aboard were struck with fear and dread; but the mermaid still sat peacefully on her floating iceberg and calmly watched the violet flashes of lightning zigzagging down into the glittering sea.

The first time each of the sisters rose above the surface, she was enchanted by all the new and wonderful sights, but now that the five were old enough to journey up whenever they liked, they soon lost interest; after a short time at the surface, they longed to be home again. The most beautiful place in the world was deep beneath the sea.

Still, there were many evenings when the five sisters would link arms and rise to the surface together. They had lovely voices—no human voice was ever so hauntingly beautiful—and when a storm blew up and they thought that a ship might be wrecked, they would swim in front of the vessel and sing about the delights of their world beneath the sea: the sailors should have no fear of coming there. But the sailors never understood the songs; they fancied they were hearing the sound of the storm. Nor could they ever see for themselves the paradise down below, for when the ship sank, they were drowned, and only drowned men ever reached the mer-king's palace.

On those evenings, the youngest would be left behind all alone, gazing after them. She would have cried, but a mermaid has no tears—and that makes her feel more grief than if she did.

And then at last she was fifteen.

"There, now! We're getting you off our hands at last!" said her grandmother, the old queen mother. "Come along, and let me dress you up like your sisters." And on the girl's head she put a wreath of white lilies, but every petal was really half a pearl.

"Goodbye," the little mermaid said, and she floated up through the water as lightly as a bubble.

The sun had just set when her head touched the surface, but the clouds still had a gleam of

63

gold and rose. Up in the pale-pink sky, the evening star shone out, clear and radiant; the air was soft and mild, and the sea was calm as glass. A great three-masted ship was lying there. Only one sail was set, as there wasn't a breath of wind, and the sailors were idly waiting in the rigging and yardarms. There were sounds of music and singing, and as the night grew darker, hundreds of colored lanterns lit the scene; it was as if flags of all the nations were flying in the wind.

The little mermaid swam right up to a porthole. Every time she rose with the lift of the waves, she could see through the clear glass a crowd of people in splendid clothes—and the handsomest of all was a young prince with large, dark eyes. He could not have been much older than sixteen—in fact, this was his birthday, and the cause of all the excitement. Now sailors began to dance on the decks, and when the young prince stepped out among them, more than a hundred rockets shot up in the air. They made the night as bright as day, so that the little mermaid was quite terrified and dived down under  the water. But she soon popped her head up again, and then she thought all the stars of heaven were falling down toward her. She had never seen fireworks. Catherine wheels were spinning around like suns, rockets like fiery fish soared into the sky, and all this was reflected in the sea. On the ship itself there was so much light that you could make out the smallest rope and the features of every face. Oh, how handsome the young prince was! There he stood, shaking hands with one guest after another, laughing and smiling, while the music rang out into the night.

It was growing late, but the little mermaid could not take her eyes from the ship and the handsome prince. The colored lamps were put out; no more rockets flew up; no more guns were fired. Yet deep down in the sea, there was a murmuring and a rumbling. The waves rose higher; great clouds massed together; lightning flashed in the distance—a terrible storm was on the way. And so the crew took in sail as the great ship tossed about. The waves rose like huge black mountains, higher than the masts themselves, but the ship dived down like a swan between the billows and then rode up again on the towering crests. To the little mermaid all this was delightful—but it was no joke to the sailors. The vessel creaked and cracked, its thick planks bent under the pounding blows of the waves, the mast snapped in the middle—and then the ship heeled over on its side and water came rushing into the hold. Now at last the little mermaid

realized they were in danger; even she herself had to look out for the broken beams and planks that were churning about in the water. At one moment it was so pitch black that she could see nothing at all; then, when lightning flashed, it was so bright that she could distinguish everyone onboard. They all seemed to be desperately trying to save their own lives, but she looked about for only one—the young prince. And just as the ship broke up, she saw him, sinking down, drawn below into the deep heart of the sea.

For a moment she felt nothing but joy, for he would be coming into her own country, but then she remembered that humans could not live in the water and that only as a drowned man could he ever enter her father's palace. No, he must not die! So she swam out through the drifting, jostling beams; they could have crushed her, but the thought never entered her head. Then, diving deep into the water and rising up high with the waves, she at last reached the young prince, who could scarcely keep afloat in the raging sea any longer. His arms and legs were almost too weak to move, his beautiful eyes were closed, and he would certainly have drowned if the little mermaid had not come. She held his head above the water and let the waves carry the two of them where they would.

When morning came, the storm was over but not a trace of the ship was to be seen. The sun rose, flame red and brilliant, out of the water, and seemed to bring a tinge of life to the pale face of the prince; but his eyes remained shut. The mermaid kissed his forehead and stroked back his wet hair. The thought came to her that he was very much like the marble statue in her own little garden, and she kissed him again. Oh, if only he would live!

And now she saw dry land in front of her, and high blue mountains whose tops were white with snow. Not far from the shore were lovely green woods, and before them stood a church, or abbey — she did not know what to call it, but a building of that kind. Orange and lemon trees grew in its garden, and tall palms by the gate. Nearby, the sea formed a little bay: very calm and still, but deep, with cliffs all around where fine white sand had piled up. She swam to this bay with the handsome prince and laid him on the sand, in the warmth of the sun, taking care that his head lay well away from the sea.

The bells rang out in the great white building. So the little mermaid swam farther out and hid behind some rocks rising out of the water, covering herself in sea foam so that no one would notice her. From there she watched to see who would come to rescue the poor prince lying in the sand. Quite soon a young girl appeared. The sight of the half-drowned figure seemed to frighten her, but only for a moment. Then she went and fetched other people, and the mermaid saw the prince revive and smile at everybody around him. But he did not turn and smile at her, for of course he had no idea that she was the one who had saved him. She felt terribly sad, and after he had been taken into

the building, she dived down sorrowfully into the water and returned to her father's palace.

She had always been quiet and thoughtful, but now she became much more so. Her sisters asked what she had seen on her first journey into the human world, but she told them nothing.

On many evenings, and many mornings, she glided up to the place where she had left the prince. She saw the fruit grow ripe in the garden, and she saw it gathered in; she saw the snow melt on the high mountains — but she never saw the prince. Her one comfort was to sit in her little garden clasping her arms around the beautiful marble statue that was so much like the prince. But she no longer tended her flowers, and they grew like wild things, trailing over the paths, weaving their long stems and leaves in and out of the boughs of the trees until the whole place was in shadow.

At last she could bear it no longer, and told the story to one of her sisters; very soon the others knew it, too — nobody else, of course, except one or two other mermaids, who told only their best friends. One of these was able to tell her who the young prince was and where his kingdom lay.

"Come, little sister," said the other princesses. And then, with their arms over one another's shoulders, they rose to the surface and floated in a long row just in front of the prince's palace. It was built of a shining gold-colored stone with great marble steps, some leading right down into the sea. Towering above the roof were magnificent golden domes, and between the pillars surrounding the building stood marble statues; they almost seemed alive. Through the glass of the tall windows, you could see into splendid halls, hung with priceless silken curtains and tapestries. In the center of the largest hall, a great fountain was playing, the water leaping as high as the glass dome in the roof. The sun's rays shone through the dome, lighting the fountain and the lovely plants that grew in the great pool below.

Now that the little mermaid knew where the young prince lived, she would rise to the surface and watch there, night after night. She would swim much closer to land than any of the others had ever dared; she even went right up the narrow canal under the marble balcony, which cast its long shadow over the water. There she would sit and gaze at the young prince, who believed that he was quite alone in the moonlight.

Often in the evenings, she would see him setting out in his splendid boat with its flying flags, while music played. She would peep out from between the green rushes, and people who saw a silvery flash thought that it was only a swan spreading its wings. Many a time, later in the night, when the fishermen waited out at sea with their fiery torches, she heard them saying much that was good about the young prince; this always made her glad that she had saved his life when he lay almost dead on the waves. But he knew nothing at all about that.

She felt closer and closer to human people, and longed more and more to go up and join them. There was so much that she wished to know, but her sisters could not answer her questions. So she asked her old grandmother; *she* knew quite a few things about the upper world, as she very properly called the lands above the sea.

"If humans are not drowned, can they live forever?" asked the little mermaid. "Do they never die, as we do here in the sea?"

"Yes, indeed," said the old lady. "They, too, have to die, and their lives are even shorter than ours. We can live for three hundred years, but when our time comes to an end, we are only foam on the water—we are like the green rushes. But humans have a soul that lives on after the body has turned to dust. It flies up through the sky to the shining stars. Just as we rise out of the sea and gaze at the human world, they rise up to unknown places that we shall never reach."

"Why, I would give all my hundreds of years in exchange for being a human, even for just one day, if I then had the chance of a place in the heavenly world," said the little mermaid sadly.

"You mustn't think such things!" said the old lady. "We are much happier here, and much better off, too, than the folk up there."

"But is there nothing I can do to get an immortal soul?" asked the little mermaid.

"No," said the old lady. "Only if a human being loved you so dearly that you were more to him than father or mother; only if he clung to you with all his heart and soul, letting the priest place his right hand in yours, promising to be true to you, here and in all eternity — then you, too, would share the human destiny. But that can never happen. The very thing that is so beautiful here in the sea — I mean your mermaid's tail — they think quite ugly up there on land. Their taste is so peculiar that they have to have two clumsy props called legs if they want to look elegant."

That made the little mermaid sigh and look sadly at her fish's tail.

"Let us be cheerful," said the old lady. "Let us make the best of the three hundred years of our life by leaping and dancing — it's a good long time, after all. Then when it's over, we can have our fill of sleep; it will be all the more welcome and agreeable. Tonight, we'll have a court ball."

This was something far more splendid than any we see on land. The walls and ceilings of the great ballroom were of crystal glass, thick but perfectly clear. Several hundred enormous shells, rose red and emerald green, were set in rows on either side, each holding a bluish flame; these lit up the whole room and shone out through the walls, giving a sapphire

69

glow to the sea outside. Countless fish, large and small, could be seen swimming toward the glass, some with scales of glowing violet, others silver and gold.

Through the middle of the ballroom flowed a broad swift stream, and on it mermen and mermaids danced to a marvelous sound: the sound of their own singing. No humans have such beautiful voices—and the sweetest singer of all was the little mermaid. When she sang, the whole assembly clapped their hands; for a moment she felt a thrill of joy, for she knew that she had the most beautiful voice of all who live on land or in the sea. But she could not forget the handsome prince, and could not forget that she had no immortal soul. And so she slipped out of her father's palace and sat in her little garden, thinking her sad thoughts.

Suddenly, echoing down through the water, she heard the sound of horn music. "Ah, he must be sailing up there," she mused, "the one whom I love more than father and mother, the one who is never out of my thoughts. To win his love and to gain an immortal soul, I would dare anything! Yes—while my sisters are dancing in our father's palace, I will call on the old sea witch. I have always been dreadfully afraid of her, but she may be able to tell me what to do."

And so the little mermaid left her garden and set off for the roaring whirlpools, for the old enchantress lived just beyond. She had never taken that grim path before; no flowers grew there, no sea grass, even. All she could see was bare gray sand stretching away from the whirlpool, where the water went swirling around as if huge, crazy millwheels were always turning, dragging everything caught in them down, down into unknown depths. To reach the sea witch's domain, she had to go right through these raging waters, and after that there was no other way but over a long swampy stretch of bubbling mud—the witch called it her peat bog. Behind this lay her house, deep in an eerie forest. The trees and bushes were of the polymorphous kind, half creature and half plant; they looked like hundred-headed snakes growing out of the ground. The branches were really long, slimy arms with fingers like writhing worms; from joint to joint they never stopped moving, and everything they could touch they twined around and held in a lasting grip.

The little mermaid was terrified as she stood on the edge of this frightful forest. She almost turned back—but then she thought of the prince and the human soul, and plucked up courage. She tied her long, flowing hair tightly around her head to keep it from the clutch of the worm-fingers; then, folding her hands together, she darted along as a fish darts through the water, in and out of the hideous branches, which reached out their waving arms and fingers after her.

Now she came to a large, slimy, open space in the dreadful forest, where fat water snakes were frisking about, showing their ugly yellow-white undersides—the sea witch called these her little pets. In the very middle, a house had been built from the bones of shipwrecked humans, and here sat the witch herself.

"I know well enough why you are here," said the witch. "It's a foolish notion! However, you shall have your way, for it will bring you nothing but trouble, my pretty princess! You want to get rid of your fish's tail and have two stumps instead, like human beings; then, you hope, the young prince will fall in love with you, and you'll be able to marry him and get an immortal soul in the bargain." With that, the witch uttered such a loud and horrible laugh that the creatures coiling over her fell sprawling to the ground.

"You've come just in the nick of time," said the witch. "Tomorrow, after sunrise, I wouldn't be able to help for another year. Now I shall make a special potion for you; before the sun rises, you must swim with it to the land, sit down, and drink it up. Then your tail will divide in two and shrink into what those humans call a lovely pair of legs. But it'll hurt; it will be like a sharp sword going through you. Everyone will say that you are the loveliest child they have ever seen. You will glide along — ah, more gracefully than any dancer — but every step you take will be like treading on a sharp knife. If you are willing to suffer all this, then I will help you."

"Yes, I am willing," said the little mermaid. Her voice trembled, but she fixed her thoughts on the prince, and the chance to gain an immortal soul.

"But remember," said the witch, "when once you've taken a human shape, you can never again be a mermaid. You can never go down through the water to your sisters, or to your father's palace! And if you fail to win the prince's love, so that he forgets both father and mother for your sake and lets the priest join you together as man and wife, you won't get that immortal soul. On the first morning after he marries another, your heart will break and you will turn into foam on the water."

"I am willing," said the little mermaid. She was now as pale as death.

"But I want my payment, too," said the witch. "And it's not a small one, either. You have the most exquisite voice of anyone here in the sea. You

think that you will be able to charm him with it, but you're going to give that voice to me. The price of my precious drink is the finest thing you possess, for I shall have to put some of my own blood into it, to make it as sharp as a two-edged sword."

"But if you take my voice," said the little mermaid, "what shall I have left?"

"Your beauty," said the witch, "your grace in moving, your lovely, speaking eyes — with these you can easily catch a human heart. Well, have you lost your courage? Put out your little tongue; I'll cut it off as my payment, and you shall have the magic drink."

"Well, if it must be so," said the little mermaid, and the witch put her cauldron on the fire to prepare the potion.

"Cleanliness is a good thing," she remarked, and she wiped out the cauldron with a knotted bunch of snakes. Then she scratched her breast and let some black blood drip down into the pot. The steam rose up in the weirdest shapes, enough to fill anyone with fear and dread. Every moment the witch cast some different item into the cauldron, and when it was really boiling, it sounded like the weeping of a crocodile. At last the brew was ready — and it looked like the clearest water.

"There you are!" said the witch, and she cut off the little mermaid's tongue. Now she had no voice; she could neither sing nor speak.

"If those trees catch hold of you when you are going back through the wood," said the witch, "just throw a drop of the potion on them. You'll see!" But the little mermaid had no need to do that, for the trees drew back in fear when they saw the potion glittering in her hand like a star. So she came back without delay through the swamp, the forest, and the roaring whirlpool.

She could see her father's palace; the lights were out in the great ballroom—no doubt they were all asleep by now. Yet she dared not go and look, for she could not speak and she was about to leave them forever. She felt as if her heart would break with grief. She crept into the garden, took one flower from the flower bed of each sister, threw a thousand kisses toward the palace, and rose up through the dark-blue sea.

The sun had not yet risen when she came in sight of the prince's palace and made her way up the splendid marble steps. The moon was shining bright and clear. The little mermaid drank the burning drink. A two-edged sword seemed to thrust itself through her delicate body; she fainted, and lay as though dead.

When the sun rose, shining across the sea, she woke, and the sharp pain returned, but there in front of her stood the young prince. His jet-black eyes were fixed on her so intently that she cast her own eyes down—and then she saw that the fish's tail was gone, and that she had instead the prettiest neat white legs that any girl could wish for. But she had no clothes, and so she wrapped herself in her long, flowing hair.

The prince asked who she was, and how she had come there, but she could only gaze back at him sweetly and sadly with her deep-blue eyes, for of course she could not speak. Then he took her by the hand and led

her into the palace. Every step she took made her feel as if she were treading on pointed swords, just as the witch had warned her — yet she endured it gladly. Holding the prince's hand, she trod the ground, light as air, and the prince and all who saw her marveled at her graceful, gliding walk.

She was given rich dresses of the finest silk and muslin. All agreed that she was the loveliest maiden in the palace.

But she was mute; she could neither sing nor speak. Beautiful slave girls in silk and gold came forward to sing for the prince and his royal parents. One of them sang more movingly than the rest, and the prince clapped his hands and smiled at her. This saddened the little mermaid, for she knew that her own lost voice was far more beautiful. She thought, *If only he could know that I gave away my voice forever, just to be near him.*

Next the slave girls danced in a graceful, gliding motion to thrilling music, and then the little mermaid rose onto the tips of her toes and floated across the floor, dancing as no one had ever yet danced. With every movement she seemed lovelier, and her eyes spoke more deeply to the heart than all the slave girls' singing.

The whole court was delighted, and the prince most of all; he called her his little foundling. So she went on dancing, though every time her feet touched the ground, she seemed to be treading on sharp knives. The prince declared that she must never leave him, and she was given a place to sleep outside his door on a velvet cushion.

He had a boy's suit made for her so that she could go riding with him on horseback. They rode through the sweet-smelling woods, where the green boughs touched her shoulders and the little birds twittered away in the fresh green leaves. She joined the prince when he climbed high mountains, and though her delicate feet were cut for all to see, she only laughed and

kept at his side until they could see the clouds sailing beneath them like a flock of birds on the way to distant lands.

At night in the prince's palace, when the others were all asleep, she would go out to the wide marble steps and cool her burning feet in the cold seawater; then she would think of those down below in the depths of the waves.

One night, her sisters rose to the surface, arm in arm, singing mournfully as they swam across the water; she waved to them and they recognized her, and told her how unhappy she had made them all. After that, they would visit her every night. Once, in the far distance, she perceived her old grandmother, who hadn't been to the surface for years, together with the mer-king himself, wearing his crown. They both stretched out their hands toward her, but they would not venture as near to land as her sisters.

As each day passed, the prince grew fonder and fonder of the little mermaid. He loved her as one loves a dear good child, but the idea of making her his queen never entered his head. And yet, if she did not become his wife, she would never gain an immortal soul, and on his wedding morning to another she would dissolve into foam on the sea.

"Do you not love me more than all the rest?" her eyes seemed to say when he took her in his arms and kissed her delicate forehead.

"Yes, of course, you are dearest of all to me," said the prince, "because you have the truest heart of all. Besides, you also remind me of a young girl I once saw — and doubt if I shall ever see again. I was on a ship that was wrecked, and the waves drove me to land near a sacred temple, which was tended by many young maidens. The youngest of them found me on the beach and saved my life. I saw her twice, no more, but she was the only one I could ever love in this world, and you are so like her that you almost take her place in my heart. But she belongs to the holy temple, so it is my good fortune that you have been sent to me. We shall never part."

Ah, he doesn't know that I was the one who saved his life, thought the little mermaid. *He doesn't know that I carried him through the waves to the temple in the woods, that I waited in the foam to see if anyone would come to rescue him, and that I saw the beautiful maiden whom he loves more than me.* The mermaid sighed deeply — though weep she could not. "The maiden belongs to the holy temple" — those had been his words. She will never come out into the world, so they will not meet again. I am here; I am with him; I see him every day. I will care for him, love him, give up my life for him!

But now the rumor rose that the prince was to be married to the lovely daughter of the neighboring king and that because of this he was outfitting a splendid ship. "The prince is supposed to be traveling forth to visit the next-door kingdom," people said. "But it's really to call on the king's daughter." The little mermaid shook her head and laughed: she knew the prince's mind better than anyone. "I am obliged to make this journey," he had said to her. "I have to meet the charming princess — my mother and father insist on that, but they cannot force me to bring her home as my bride. I cannot love this stranger! She will not remind me of the fair maid of the temple, as you do. If I have to find a bride, my choice  would be you, my dear, mute foundling with the speaking eyes." And he kissed her rose-red mouth.

"You have no fear of the sea, my silent child!" he said as they stood on the splendid ship that was to carry him to the lands of the neighboring king. And he told her of storms and calm, of strange fish in the deep and the marvels that divers had seen down there; she smiled at his accounts, for of course she knew more about the world beneath the waves than anyone.

In the moonlit night, when everyone but the helmsman at the wheel was asleep, she sat by the ship's rail, gazing into the calm water. She thought that she could make out her father's palace, with her old grandmother standing on the highest tower, in her silver crown, peering up through the racing tides at the vessel overhead. Then her sisters came to the surface and looked at her with eyes full of sorrow, wringing their white hands. She waved to them and smiled, and wanted to tell them that all was going well and happily with her, but then one of the cabin boys drew near, and her sisters sank below.

Next morning the ship sailed into the harbor of the neighboring king's fine city. All the church bells were ringing; trumpets blared from the tall towers, while soldiers stood on parade with flying flags and glinting bayonets. Every day was like a fête: No sooner was one ball or party over than another began. But the princess was not there. She was being brought up in a holy temple, they said, where she was learning the ways of wisdom that her royal role would need. At last, however, she arrived.

The little mermaid waited by, eager to see her beauty, and she had to admit that it would be hard to find a lovelier human girl. Her skin was so delicate and pure, and behind her long lashes smiled a pair of steadfast dark-blue eyes.

"It is you!" said the prince. "You were the one who saved me when I lay almost dead on the shore!" And he held the blushing princess in his arms.

"Oh, I am overjoyed," he said to the little mermaid.

"My dearest wish—more than I ever dared hope for—has come true. I know you will share in my happiness, because no one anywhere cares for me more than you." The little mermaid kissed his head, though she felt that her heart would break. His wedding morning would bring her death and turn her to a wisp of foam on the sea.

All the church bells rang out; heralds rode through the streets to proclaim the news. Sweet-smelling oils burned on every altar in precious silver lamps. The priests swung incense vessels; bride and bridegroom joined their hands and received the bishop's blessing. The little mermaid, in silk and gold, stood holding the bridal train, but her ears never heard the festive music, nor did her eyes see the holy ceremony. This was her last day alive in the world, and she was thinking of all that she had lost.

That evening the bride and bridegroom went aboard the ship. A royal tent of gold and purple had been set up on the main deck with silken cushions and hangings, and there the bridal pair were to sleep in that calm, cool, pleasant night.

The sails filled out in the breeze, and the vessel flew swiftly and lightly over the shining sea.

As darkness fell, lanterns of every color were lit, and on the deck the sailors danced merrily. The little mermaid remembered the first time she had come to the surface and had gazed on just such a joyful scene. And now she, too, was joining in the dance, lightly gliding and swerving as a swallow does to avoid a pursuer. She could hear the admiring voices and applause, for never before had she danced so brilliantly. Sharp knives seemed to cut her delicate feet, yet she hardly felt them, so deep was the pain in her heart. She could not forget that this was the last night she would ever see the one for whom she had left her home and family, had given up her beautiful voice, and had day by day endured unending torment, of which he knew nothing at all. An eternal night awaited her.

At last, well after midnight, the merrymaking drew to a close. The prince kissed his lovely bride, and they went to the royal tent. The ship grew hushed and silent; only the helmsman was still awake at the wheel. The little mermaid leaned her white arms on the rail and looked eastward for a sign of the dawn; the first ray of the sun, she knew, would mean her end. Suddenly, rising out of the sea, she saw her sisters. They were as ghastly pale as she, and their beautiful hair no longer streamed in the wind — it had been cut off.

"We gave our hair to the witch in return for help, for something that will save you from death when morning breaks. She has given us a knife. Look! See how sharp it is! Before the sun rises, you must plunge it into the prince's heart; when his warm blood splashes your feet, they will grow together into a fish's tail and you will become a mermaid once again, just as you used to be. You will be able to join us in the depths below and live out all your three hundred years before you dissolve away into salt sea foam. Hurry! Either he or you must die before the first ray of sunrise! Our old grandmother is so full of grief that her white hair has fallen out, just as ours fell before the witch's scissors. Kill the prince and come back to us! Hurry! Do you see that red streak in the sky? In a few minutes the sun will rise and you will be no more." And with a strange, deep sigh, they sank beneath the waves.

The little mermaid drew back the purple curtain from the tent door where the prince and princess slept; she looked up at the sky where the red of dawn began to glow, looked at the sharp knife, and looked again at the prince. The knife quivered in her hand — then she flung it far out into the waves; they shone red where it fell, as though drops of blood were leaping out of the water. Once more she looked at the prince, through eyes half-glazed in death, then she threw herself from the ship into the sea, where she felt her body dissolving into foam.

And now the sun rose from the ocean, and on the foam its beams lay gentle and warm. The little mermaid had no feeling of death. She saw the bright sun and also, floating above her, hundreds of lovely transparent creatures. Through them she could see the white sails of the ship and the rose-red clouds in the sky. Their voices were like music, but of so ethereal a kind that no human ear could hear them, just as no earthly eye could perceive them. Without wings they floated through the air, borne by their own lightness. And now the little mermaid saw that she had become like them, and was rising higher and higher above the waves.

"Where am I going?" said she, and her voice, too, sounded like those of the other beings, so ethereal that no earthly music could even echo its tune.

"To join with us, spirits of the air," they answered. "We do not need the love of a human being to become immortal. We fly to hot countries where the stifling breath of plague carries death to humans, and we bring them cool, fresh breezes; we fill the air with the scent of flowers that bring relief and healing. When we have tried to do all the good we can for three hundred years, we gain an immortal soul and eternal happiness. You, too, poor little mermaid, have striven with all your heart to do good; you have suffered and endured and have raised yourself into the higher world of the spirits of the air. Now you, too, can gain an immortal soul for yourself."

The little mermaid lifted her arms toward the heavenly sun. On the ship, the bustle of waking life had started again. She saw the prince with his beautiful bride; they were searching for her, gazing sorrowfully into the moving waves. She smiled at the prince, and then, with the other children of the air, she soared up onto the rose-red cloud that floated in the sky.

"In this way, when three hundred years are passed, I shall rise into the kingdom of heaven."

"Perhaps even sooner," one of them whispered. "Unseen, we glide into human homes where there are children, and whenever we find a good child, one who makes its parents happy and deserves their love, God shortens our time of trial. The child never knows when we fly through the room; if its goodness makes us smile with pleasure, a year is taken from the three hundred. But if we see a naughty, evil child, then we must weep tears of sorrow, and each tear adds one day more to our time of waiting."

The Steadfast Tin Soldier

*F*irst published in 1838, this is the first invented fairy tale to have a non-human lead (hero or non-hero) acting out its human theme. A landmark! Andersen's invention is today a basic element of worldwide children's literature. Do writers know this ancestry?

The tale itself is a model of storytelling. With its pace, its verve, its detail, even the soldier's thoughts, it seems (and is) perfectly aimed at children. But serious tributes have also come from adults — among them the Nobel Prize–winning novelist Thomas Mann and the Grand Duchess of Weimar. She turned to the tale, she said, for courage when facing childbirth.

How much of Andersen himself is in the story? The main link is that the soldier, too, is a loner, an outsider (with his single leg), the only one to escape the crowded wooden box and learn for himself the hazards of his world. And what chance has he with the little paper dancer? In any case, what home could he offer a wife? "I have only a box, and there are twenty-five of us in that!"

Odd items, though, are plentiful. The paper castle and dancer are reminiscent of Andersen's own paper-and-scissors handiwork — paper-cutting being one of his special skills. The passport episode? It is a familiar Andersen situation. And the end? A sad affair or a triumph? Read the story's final paragraph again, and you should have no doubts. The soldier even has his wish — where else but in this fiery place could the patient lovers ever have met? A sad affair or a triumph? The price was high, soaringly high, but a triumph surely.

THERE WERE ONCE TWENTY-FIVE TIN SOLDIERS; they were all brothers, for they had all been made from the same tin kitchen spoon. Very smart in their red-and-blue uniforms, they shouldered arms and looked straight before them.

"Tin soldiers!" Those were the first words they heard in this world, when the lid of their box was taken off. A little boy had shouted this and clapped his hands; they were a birthday present, and now he set them out on the table. Each soldier was exactly like the next, except for one who had only a single leg: he had been the last to be molded, and there had not been quite enough tin left. Yet he stood just as well on his one leg as the others did on their two — and he is this story's hero.

On the table where they were placed there were many other toys, but the one that everyone noticed first was a paper castle, the rooms of which you could see right into through its little windows. At the front some tiny trees were arranged around a piece of mirror, just like a lake; swans made of wax seemed to float on its surface, gazing at their reflections.

The whole effect was quite enchanting — but the prettiest thing in the entire scene was a young girl who stood in the castle's open doorway. She, too, was cut out of paper, but her gauzy skirt was of finest muslin; a narrow blue ribbon crossed her shoulder like a scarf and was held with a

86

glittering spangle that was nearly the size of her face. This charming little creature held both of her arms stretched out, for she was a dancer; indeed, one of her legs was raised so high that the tin soldier could not see it at all. He believed that she had only one leg, like himself.

Now, she would be just the right wife for me, he thought. *But she is so grand. She lives in a castle and I have only a box, and there are twenty-five of us in that! It's certainly no place for her. Still, I can try to make her acquaintance.* So he lay down full-length behind a snuffbox that was on the table; from there he had a good view of the little paper dancer, who continued to stand on one leg without losing her balance.

When evening came, all the other tin soldiers were put in their box, and the people of the house went to bed. Now the toys began to have games of their own; they played at visiting, and battles, and going to parties and dances. The tin soldiers rattled in their box, for they wanted to join in, but they couldn't get the lid off. The nutcrackers turned somersaults, and the slate pencil squeaked on the slate; there was such a din that the canary woke up and joined in the talk — what's more, he did it in verse. The only two who didn't move from their places were the tin soldier and the little dancer. She continued to stand on the point of her toe; he stood just as steadily on his single leg, and never once did he take his eyes from her.

Now the clock struck twelve. *Crack!* The lid flew off the snuffbox, and a little goblin popped up. There was no snuff inside—it was a toy, a jack-in-the-box.

"Tin soldier!" screeched the goblin. "Keep your eyes to yourself!" But the tin soldier pretended not to hear.

"All right, just you wait till tomorrow!" warned the goblin.

When morning came, and the children were up again, the little boy put the tin soldier on the windowsill. The goblin may have been responsible, or perhaps a draft was blowing through—anyhow, the window suddenly swung open and out fell the tin soldier, all three stories to the ground.

It was a dreadful fall! His leg pointed upward, his head was down, and he came to a halt with his bayonet stuck between the paving stones.

The servant girl and the small boy went out at once to look for the tin soldier, but although they were almost treading on him, they didn't see him. If he had called out, "Here I am!" they would have found him easily, but he didn't think it proper behavior to cry out when in uniform.

It began to rain; the drops fell faster and faster—it was a real drenching storm. When it was over, a pair of street urchins passed. "Look!" said one of them. "There's a tin soldier! Let's put him out to sea."

So they made a boat of newspaper, put the tin soldier aboard, and set the boat in the fast-flowing gutter at the edge of the street. Away it sped, and the two boys ran along beside, clapping their hands. Goodness! What waves there were in that gutter stream, what rolling tides! The paper boat tossed up and down, sometimes whirling around and around, until the soldier felt quite giddy. But he remained as steadfast as

88

ever, not moving a muscle, still looking straight in front of him, still shouldering arms.

All at once the boat entered a tunnel under the pavement. Oh, it was dark, as dark as in the box at home. *Wherever am I going now?* the tin soldier wondered. *Yes, it must be the goblin's doing. Ah, if only that young lady were sharing this journey with me, I wouldn't care if it were twice as dark!*

Suddenly a large water rat rushed out from its home in the tunnel. "Have you a passport?" the rat demanded. "No getting through without a passport!"

But the tin soldier said never a word; he only gripped his musket more tightly than ever. The boat rushed on and the rat chased after it. Ugh! How it ground its teeth as it yelled to the sticks and straws, "Stop him! Stop him! He hasn't paid his toll! He hasn't shown his passport!"

There was no stopping him, though, for the stream ran stronger and stronger. The tin soldier could see a bright glimpse of daylight ahead, where the end of the tunnel must be, but at the same time he heard a roaring noise that might have frightened a bolder man. Just imagine! At the end of the tunnel, the stream thundered down into a canal. It was as fearful a ride for him as a plunge down a giant waterfall would be for us.

But he was already so near to the edge that he

could not stop. The boat raced on, and the poor tin soldier held himself as stiffly as he could. No one could say of him that he even blinked an eye. All at once the little vessel whirled around three or four times and filled with water to the brim. What could it do but sink? The tin soldier stood in water

up to his neck; deeper and deeper sank the boat, softer and softer grew the paper, until at last the water closed over the soldier's head. He thought of the lovely little dancer whom he would never see again, and in his ears rang the words of a song:

> *Onward, onward, warrior,*
> *Meet thy fate; show no fear.*

Then the paper boat collapsed altogether. Out fell the tin soldier — and he was at once swallowed up by a fish. Oh, how dark it was in the fish's stomach! It was even worse than the tunnel, and much more cramped. But the tin soldier's courage was quite unchanged; there he lay, steadfast as ever,

his musket still on his shoulder. The fish swam wildly to and fro, twisted and turned, and then became still. Something flashed through like a streak of lightning — then all around was cheerful daylight. A voice cried out, "The tin soldier!"

The fish had been caught, taken to market, sold, and carried into the kitchen, where the cook had cut it open with a large knife. Now she picked up the soldier, holding him around his waist between her finger and thumb, and took him into the living room, so that all the family could see and admire the remarkable character who had traveled back in a fish.

But the tin soldier was not proud; he thought nothing of it.

They stood him up on the table, and there — well, the world is full of wonders: He saw that he was in the very same room where his adventures had started; there were the same children; there were the

same toys; there was the fine paper castle with the graceful little dancer at the door. She was still poised on one leg, with the other raised high in the air. Ah, she was steadfast, too. The tin soldier was deeply moved; he would have liked to weep tin tears, only that would not have been soldierly behavior. He looked at her and she looked at him, but not a word passed between them.

And then a strange thing happened. One of the small boys picked up the tin soldier and threw him into the stove. He had no reason for doing this; it must have been the fault of the snuffbox goblin.

The tin soldier stood framed in a blaze of light. The heat was intense, but whether this came from the fire or from his burning love he could not tell. His bright colors were now completely gone, but whether they had faded on the journey or through his sorrow, none could say. He looked at the little dancer, and she looked at him — he felt that he was melting, but he still stood steadfast, shouldering arms. Suddenly the door flew open, a gust of air caught the pretty little paper dancer, and she flew like a sylph right into the stove, straight to the waiting tin soldier; there she flashed into flames and was gone.

Soon the soldier melted down to a lump of tin, and the next day, when the maid raked out the ashes, she found him — in the shape of a little tin heart. And what remained of the dancer?

Only her spangle, and that was black as soot. ⤙

The Wild Swans

*T*he Wild Swans" (1837) was one of the rare Andersen tales to be based on a familiar traditional theme from Grimm and other sources. In the Grimms' much shorter version, the swans are six to Andersen's eleven, the needless details few.

What drew Andersen to this story? For a start, here was a heroine to his liking—a young girl choosing to endure a long and harrowing act of sacrifice to break an evil spell. The swans, for him, were the noblest of birds, yet outcasts, as he saw himself until he won his fame.

But possibly the greatest lure of all was the enjoyable chance that the wide range of the story gave for his special gifts as a writer and storyteller. Descriptions? Take Elisa's magical summer sojourn in the woods, for instance. Drama? Will the swans reach the tiny mid-ocean rock in time? Or turn too soon into humans and plummet to their deaths?

But the peak of imagination is in the great flight through the clouds. Scene after marvelous scene appears to Elisa in the all-too-soon dissolving cloudscapes. "That one," the swans tell her, "was the cloud palace of the fairy Morgana: lovely, but ever-changing; no mortal might enter there." You won't find this in Grimm. Aerial flight was something that Andersen longed to experience. He wrote it into a number of his stories, but never so memorably as here.

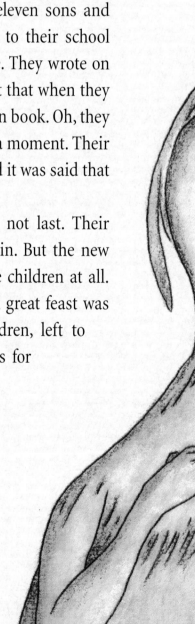

*F*AR, FAR AWAY, IN THE LAND where the swallows fly during our winter, there lived a king. He had eleven sons and a daughter, Elisa. The eleven young princes went to their school each wearing a star at his heart and a sword at his side. They wrote on leaves of gold with diamond pencils, and learned so fast that when they gave answers they might have been reading from an open book. Oh, they were fairy-tale princes all right — you could tell that in a moment. Their sister, Elisa, sat on a little stool made of mirror glass, and it was said that her picture book had cost half a kingdom.

Yes, they lived royally, those children. But this did not last. Their mother being dead, their father, the king, married again. But the new queen was evil, and she did not care for the children at all. They discovered this on her very first day. A great feast was held to celebrate her arrival, and the children, left to themselves, decided to play at having guests for tea. But instead of the cakes and roasted apples that they were usually given, the new queen allowed them only a cupful of sand. "You can pretend that this is your feast," they were told.

A week later she sent little Elisa off into the country to live with a peasant family. Then, before long, she managed to fill the king's mind with such shocking tales about the poor young princes that he wished to have nothing more to do with them. "Out you go!" said the wicked woman to the boys. "Fend for yourselves as you may. Fly off as voiceless birds!"

Yet she could not do as much harm as she intended, for they turned into eleven beautiful wild swans, each wearing a golden crown. With a strange cry they flew out of the palace window, over the great gardens, the fields and woods, into the unknown. Early in the morning they passed the place where their sister, Elisa, had been sent. They circled around the cottage roof, flapping their wings, craning their necks, but nobody heard or saw them. At last they had to fly on, through the clouds, into the wide world.

Poor little Elisa sat in the cottage playing with a green leaf—the only toy she had. She pricked a hole in it and peeped through at the sunlight. The brightness made her think of the bright eyes of her brothers.

Time passed, one day like another. But whenever the wind blew through the garden, it would say to the roses, "Who could be more beautiful than you?" And the roses would reply, "Elisa is more beautiful." What they said was the truth.

When Elisa was fifteen, she was brought back to the palace. The evil queen, seeing how lovely she had become, was extremely vexed. Indeed, she would have promptly turned the girl into a bird, like her brothers, but she did not dare—not just yet—since the king wished to see his daughter.

Early next morning, the queen went into Elisa's bathroom with three toads. She kissed the first and said, "Hop onto Elisa's head and make her as slow and dull as you." She kissed the second and said, "Make her look as ugly as you, so that her father will not know her!" Then she kissed the

third and whispered, "Fill her with evil, so that she knows no peace." She put the toads into the clear water, which at once took on a strange greenish tinge. Yet Elisa seemed to notice nothing. And when she rose from the water, no toads were there, only three floating poppies. If the toads had not been poisoned by the wicked queen's kiss, they would have become red roses — Elisa's touch alone had made them flowers.

When the queen perceived her failure, she planned again. This time she rubbed Elisa's skin with dark-brown walnut juice and made her hair look wild and tangled. You wouldn't have recognized her! And so, when her father saw her, he was shocked. "That is not my daughter!" he declared. No one else at court would have anything to do with her, except the watchdog and the garden swallows — and who ever cared about what they thought?

Poor Elisa! She started to cry, then she crept out of the palace and wandered all day over field and moor and meadow, until at day's end she found herself in a great forest. She had no idea where she was, but she fixed her mind on her brothers. They had been driven forth, like herself, and now she would go to the ends of the earth to find them.

Night fell, and she lay down on some soft moss. All was silent; the air was mild and touched with a greenish light that came from hundreds of fireflies. There were so many that when she gently touched a branch, shining creatures wafted down like a shower of tiny stars.

All that night she dreamed about her brothers. They were playing together, as they had when they were children, writing with the diamond pencils on the golden leaves. Only now, instead of playing games, like tic-tac-toe, they were writing down all that had befallen them in the missing years—bold deeds and strange adventures. She, too, was in her dream, looking at the beautiful picture book that had cost half a kingdom. Everything in it seemed to come alive: the birds sang; the people stepped out of the pages and spoke to her. But whenever she turned a page, they jumped straight back, so as not to get into the wrong picture.

When she awoke, the sun was high overhead, though she could scarcely see it through the thick overhanging leaves and branches. But where the sunbeams filtered through, there was a shimmering golden haze. The air was filled with the smell of fresh green grass; the birds flew so near that they seemed about to perch on her shoulder. She heard the splashing of water. It came, she found, from a spring that flowed into a pool, so clear that you could see the sandy bed below.

Then, looking down, she saw a face reflected in the pool. It was her own—but how grimy and strange. She dipped her hand into the water and began to clean her eyes and forehead—what a contrast! Soon her own clear skin shone through; she was herself again. She took off all her clothes and stepped into the clear, cool water. Now, even in her torn dress, a more beautiful princess could not have been found anywhere in the world.

As she set off again, she met an old woman, who gave her some berries from a basket she was carrying. Elisa asked her if she had come across eleven princes riding through the forest.

"No," said the old woman. "But yesterday I saw eleven swans with gold crowns on their heads — they were swimming down yonder river."

She led Elisa to a slope where, down below, almost hidden by arching overhead branches, was a fast-running stream. Elisa thanked the old woman and began to walk along the winding bank. The water widened out until at last it reached the sea.

Now the great ocean lay before her, but there was not a boat, not a sail in sight. It was almost nightfall; what was she to do? Then she saw, scattered among the seaweed and sea grasses, some white feathers — swans' feathers. She picked them up; there were eleven of them. She heard the sound of wings, and looked up. Eleven wild swans, each with a golden crown on its head, were flying toward the beach, one behind the other, like a long, white ribbon in the sky. Quickly hiding behind a bush, she watched them landing, flapping their great white wings.

A moment later the sun sank below the horizon. At once the swans' feathers fell away — and there stood eleven handsome princes, Elisa's brothers. She ran toward them, calling them by name. They, in turn, were overjoyed to see their little sister, and they told her their own strange tale.

"So long as the sun is in the sky," the eldest said, "we have to fly as swans. At nightfall we return to human form. But we need to be careful — we must have a landing place before sunset. If we were still flying in the air, we would, as humans, hurtle down to our deaths.

"Our true homeland is no longer our home. The land where we live now is beautiful, but it is far from here. To reach it we must cross the vast ocean, and there is no island where we can rest as humans in the night. Only one thing saves us. About halfway across, a tiny rock rises out of the water —

just large enough to hold us standing close together. When the waves are rough, we are drenched in spray, but without that rock, we would never be able to visit our beloved native country. You can understand why we need two of the longest days in the year for our flight.

"So, once a year we cross the sea and fly over the great forest and gaze at the castle where we were born and circle around the high tower of the church where our mother is buried. The wild horses gallop over the plains as they did in our childhood; the charcoal burner still sings the old songs that we danced to as children. This is our home, the land that will always draw us back, however hard the journey.

"But tomorrow we must start back for that other country—a beautiful place, but not our own. For a whole year we cannot fly here again. What will become of you, little sister?"

"I must go with you," Elisa said.

All that night the brothers, in human form, began to weave a net of willow bark and rushes, an airy chariot for Elisa. When the sun rose, and they became swans again, they picked up the net in their beaks and flew with their sister high toward the clouds. The youngest hovered just overhead to keep her from the sun's hot rays.

All the long day they flew, like arrows in the sky. Yet, swift as they were, they were slower than at other times, since they had their sister to carry. Night was near; thunder shook the air—but still no sign appeared of the tiny rock. At any moment now the brothers would return to human shape, and all would fall to their deaths. Black clouds shut out the remaining light; storm winds churned the leaden water; flash after flash of lightning pierced the gloom.

Suddenly the birds headed downward. The sun was already halfway into the sea — but now, for the first time, Elisa saw the little rock. It could have been a seal's head looking out of the water. Then she felt ground beneath her — and at that moment the sun went out like the last spark on a piece of burning paper. All around her, close together, were her brothers, humans now, sheltering her from the dashing waves.

At dawn the air was clear and still. As the sun rose, the brothers again became swans and soared from the rock with Elisa in her woven raft; there was no time to be lost before they reached land again. From far above, the white foam on the dark-green curling waves seemed to Elisa like thousands of floating swans. Then, as she looked ahead, she was amazed to see a range of mountains with glittering, icy peaks. In their midst was a mighty palace, which seemed to stretch for miles. Below were groves of waving palm  trees and wonderful flowers, vast in size, like mill wheels. Yet all this seemed to be hanging in the air. Was it the beautiful land they were making for? The swans shook their heads. What she was seeing, they told her, was the cloud palace of the fairy Morgana: lovely, but ever-changing; no mortal could enter there.

And as Elisa gazed, mountains, palace, trees, and flowers all dissolved, and in their place rose a score of noble churches with lofty towers. She thought that she heard organ music — or was it the sound of the sea? Then, when they seemed quite near, the churches changed to a fleet of ships, sailing just below. She looked again — there were no ships; all she saw was a whirl of mist over the water. Sea, air, and sky are ever in motion: no vision ever comes to the watcher twice.

At last Elisa glimpsed real land. Blue mountains of rare beauty rose up before her, and she could just perceive forests of cedar, cities and palaces. The swans alighted, and Elisa found herself at the mouth of a hillside cave, an opening almost hidden by a web of vines and other trailing greenery.

"You can rest here safely," the youngest said. "Sleep now, and have good dreams."

"If only I could dream how to set you free," she answered.

But was it a dream that came to her? She thought that she was flying through the air, straight to the cloud castle of the fairy Morgana. The fairy herself came to meet her. She was radiant and beautiful—yet she also seemed strangely like the old woman who had given her berries in the forest and had told her where to find the swans with golden crowns.

"Your brothers can be freed," said the fairy. "But have you enough courage and endurance? Look at this stinging nettle. It grows plentifully around the cave where you are sleeping, but in only one other place—on churchyard graves. Now, first you must gather some in your bare hands, though they will sting and burn your soft skin. Then you must tread on them with your bare feet until they have turned into flax. You

must twist this flax into thread, and weave this thread into cloth. From the cloth you must make eleven shirts, like coats of mail with sleeves. Throw one of these over each of your brothers, and the spell will break. But — this is important — until you finish your task, even if it takes years, you must not speak. A single word will pierce your brothers' hearts like a sword. Their lives depend on your silence. Remember!"

She touched Elisa's hand with the nettle. It scorched her skin like fire — and she awoke. She must have slept long, for it was now bright daylight. Nearby was a nettle, very much like the one she had seen in the dream. She went outside the cave; yes, there the nettles were. She would start at once. Quickly she plucked an armful, trampled them out, and began to twist the green flax into thread.

At sunset the brothers returned. At first Elisa's silence alarmed them, as did her strange work. Then they decided that all this must be linked with her wish to break the spell; her silence and toil were for their sake.

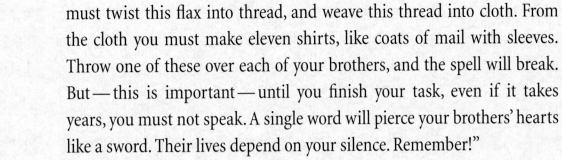

All through the night, Elisa worked. When day returned, the swan-brothers flew far afield, but though she was alone, she had never found time to go by so fast. One nettle shirt was already finished; she started on the next.

Suddenly a sound rang from the mountains, the echoing of a hunting horn. It was followed by the barking of dogs. The noise came nearer; Elisa was seized with terror, still more when a great hound sprang out of the bushes, then another and another. They made for the mouth of the cave: soon, a group of huntsmen had gathered all over her hiding place. One, the most handsome of all, stepped forward. Indeed, he was the king of that land. He gazed at Elisa; she seemed to him the most beautiful girl in the world.

"How do you come to be here?" he asked.

Elisa shook her head. She dared not speak.

"This is no place for you," said the king. "Come with me. If you are as good as you are beautiful, you shall wear a golden crown on your head, and the finest of my castles shall be your home."

He lifted her onto his horse, and they galloped away through the mountains. His companions rode behind.

It was day's end before they reached the royal city, magnificent with its domes and towers. The king led Elisa into his palace, where sparkling  fountains splashed into marble pools and the high walls and ceilings were covered with marvelous paintings. But she wept and grieved and saw nothing. Listless and pale, she let the women dress her in royal robes, twine her hair with pearls, and cover her damaged hands with fine, soft gloves.

At last they led her into the great hall. She was so dazzlingly beautiful that the whole court bowed low before her. The king broke the silence to announce that this maiden was to be his bride and queen. But the archbishop shook his head; he muttered that the forest girl must be a witch who had cast a spell on the king's heart.

Yet the king would not hear a word against her. He ordered the most melodious music to be played and the rarest dishes to be served. She was taken through sweet-scented gardens and magnificent galleries. But nothing touched her grief. Then the king showed her a little room that would be her own. It was carpeted in green and hung with wonderful green tapestries, to make it look like the cave where she had been found. On the floor lay a bundle of nettles and flax; from the ceiling hung the one shirt she had finished. A huntsman had brought these back as curiosities.

"Here you can dream yourself back to your old home," the king told her. "Now, whenever you like, you can amuse yourself by thinking of that bygone time."

When Elisa saw what was so near to her heart, she began to smile; color came back to her pale face, and she kissed the king's hand. He took her in his arms, then gave commands for all the church bells to be rung for their wedding. The lovely, voiceless, woodland girl would be queen.

The wedding day arrived. The archbishop himself had to place the crown on Elisa's head, and he pressed it down so spitefully that it hurt. But she felt a deep affection for the good and handsome king; day by day she loved him more and more. If only she could speak! But first she had to finish her task. So each night, as the king slept, she would steal from his side and go to her work in the room that was like a green cave. Six shirts were now complete—but she had no more flax. Only in the churchyard could she find the right nettles.

So at midnight, full of fear, she crept through the moonlit garden, along the great avenues, and out into the lonely streets that led to the churchyard.

What a sight met her eyes! A ring of lamias, those witches that are half serpent and half woman, sat around the largest gravestone. With their long fingers they were clawing into the earth to find fresh corpses for a feast. Elisa had to pass close by them, and they fixed their dreadful gaze upon her, but she prayed for safety, gathered the nettles, and sped back to the palace. But not unnoticed. One person had seen and followed her—the archbishop. So his suspicions were true! The new queen was a witch.

107

In the church the next day, he told the king what he had seen. The carved saints shook their heads, as if to say, "Not so! Elisa is innocent!" But the archbishop chose to take this in his own way; the saints were bearing witness against her; they were shaking their heads at her sins.

Two heavy tears rolled down the king's face, and he went home with a troubled heart. He pretended to sleep that night, but no sleep came. Day by day he became more wretched. This troubled Elisa sorely, and added to her grief about her brothers. Her tears ran onto her velvet robes and lay there like diamonds. But people saw only her beauty and her royal clothes, and wished that they were queen.

Still, her task was nearly done, for only one more shirt had to be made. The trouble was, she had no more flax, and not a single nettle. She would have to go to the churchyard for the last time. She thought with fear of the lonely midnight journey — but then she thought of her brothers.

She started out, and the king and the archbishop followed her. They saw her pass through the iron gates of the churchyard; they saw the frightful lamias on the graves. The king turned away in grief. He thought that Elisa had come to seek the company of these monsters — his own sweet forest girl, his queen.

"The people shall judge her," he decided. And this the people did. They declared Elisa a witch and ordered her to be burned at the stake.

She was taken from the splendor of the palace and cast into a dungeon, damp and dark. Instead of silken sheets and velvet pillows, the nettles and nettlework from her room were tossed in. She could have asked for no better gift. While boys outside sang jeering songs, with shouts of "Witch! Witch!" she began to work on the last of the shirts.

The archbishop had planned to spend the last few hours in prayer with her, but when he came, Elisa shook her head and pointed to the door. Her work had to be finished that night. The archbishop went away, muttering angry words.

Poor Elisa! If only she could speak! Little mice ran over the floor; they dragged the nettles toward her, doing all they could to help. A thrush sat at the bars and sang all night to give her hope.

But the news had reached her brothers, and at first light, an hour before sunrise, the eleven princes, in human form, stood at the palace gate and demanded to see the king. "Impossible!" was the answer. "The king is asleep and may not be disturbed." They begged, they pleaded, they threatened; the guards came down to see what the noise was about. At last it brought down the king himself.

At that moment the sun rose. Where were the eleven young men? Nowhere. Over the palace flew eleven wild swans.

Meanwhile, from earliest daylight, crowds of people had jostled through the city gates, all eager to see the burning of the witch. They could see her now in a cart, dragged along by a forlorn old horse. She was wearing a smock made of coarse sacking; her lovely hair hung loose about her face; her cheeks were deathly pale, but her fingers never stopped working at the last of the nettle shirts. The other ten lay at her feet. All around, the crowds mocked and yelled, "Look at the witch! What's she up to? Still at her filthy witchcraft! Get it away from her. Tear it into a thousand pieces!"

They surged forward, and were just about to destroy her precious handiwork when down flew eleven great, white swans. Beating their wings, they settled on the cart. The mob drew back in fear.

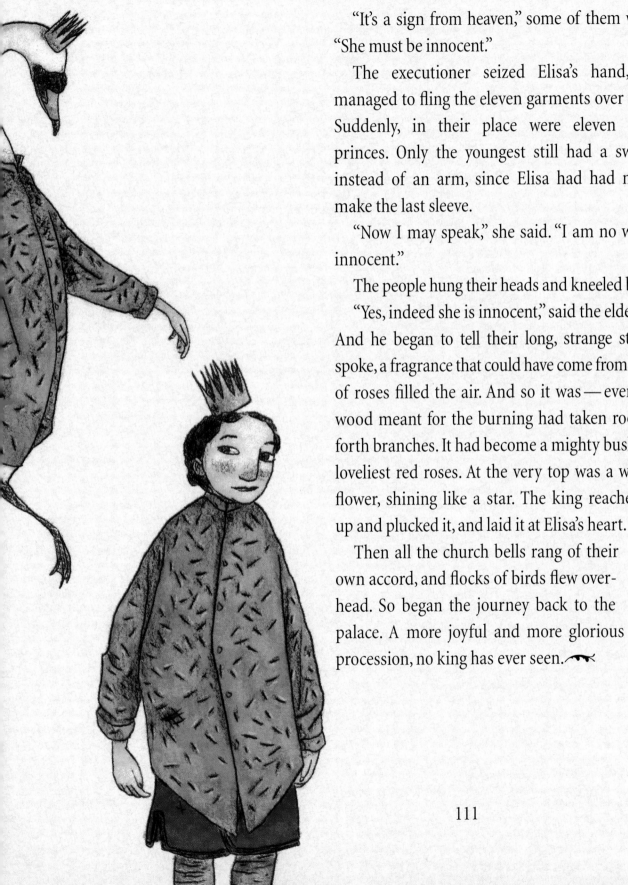

"It's a sign from heaven," some of them whispered. "She must be innocent."

The executioner seized Elisa's hand, but she managed to fling the eleven garments over the swans. Suddenly, in their place were eleven handsome princes. Only the youngest still had a swan's wing instead of an arm, since Elisa had had no time to make the last sleeve.

"Now I may speak," she said. "I am no witch. I am innocent."

The people hung their heads and kneeled before her.

"Yes, indeed she is innocent," said the eldest brother. And he began to tell their long, strange story. As he spoke, a fragrance that could have come from thousands of roses filled the air. And so it was — every piece of wood meant for the burning had taken root and put forth branches. It had become a mighty bush of the loveliest red roses. At the very top was a white flower, shining like a star. The king reached up and plucked it, and laid it at Elisa's heart.

Then all the church bells rang of their own accord, and flocks of birds flew over-head. So began the journey back to the palace. A more joyful and more glorious procession, no king has ever seen.

111

An unusually lively mood pervades this tale, with its whiff of the Arabian Nights. Why a trunk and not a horse or a carpet for the aerial flight? Well, Andersen's own traveling trunk must have caught his eye. Fair enough. Most of his stories spark into life in just this way.

But the prize of the whole is the tale within the tale, a little gem in Andersen's special genre — his invention at its best. It's a kitchen piece: kitchen items, proud or humble, voice their views, their histories. "The pot went on with her story . . . and the end was just as good as the beginning. . . . The broom took some parsley from the dustbin and put it around the pot like a crown; he knew that this would annoy the others. If I crown her today, *he thought*, she'll crown me tomorrow."

The kindly king and queen, for whom the story was composed, are delighted. But an unexpected problem has arisen. When and how, if at all, will storyteller and princess find each other again?

THERE WAS ONCE A MERCHANT who was so rich that he could have paved the whole street with silver and still had nearly enough left over for a little alleyway as well. But that isn't what he did with his money — oh, no, he had more sense. Whenever he laid out a penny, it brought him ten: that was the kind of merchant he was. And then he died.

All his money now came to his son — who lost no time in spending it. Every night he went out dancing; he made paper kites from bank notes; he

skipped stones on the lake — not with flat stones, but with gold coins. That's the way to run through money, and very soon he had nothing left but four copper coins and the clothes he had on — which were an old dressing gown and a pair of slippers. Needless to say, his friends all drifted off. Who would wish to be seen with such a ragamuffin? But one of them, more good-natured than the rest, gave him a old trunk, saying, "You'll be moving off, I fancy. That's for your belongings." All very well, but he had no belongings. So he put himself in the trunk.

It was no ordinary trunk. As soon as you pressed the lock, it rose from the ground and flew. The young man pressed the lock and — *swoosh!* — the trunk was taking him up through the chimney, over the clouds, higher and higher, farther and farther away. The bottom creaked and groaned — what if it fell out? No acrobatics could help him then. But the trunk held together, and landed at last in the country of the Turks. He hid it under some leaves in the woods and walked toward the town.

Nobody took any notice of him, because all the Turks go about in dressing gowns and slippers. He met a nursemaid with a young child. "I say, nanny," he called out, "what's the great palace just outside the city, with the windows so high in the walls?"

"Oh, that's where the king's daughter lives," she answered. "A fortune-teller has prophesied that she's going to have an unhappy love affair. So no one is allowed to visit her unless the king and queen are there as well."

"Thank you," said the merchant's son. He hurried back to the woods, stepped into his trunk, and flew up onto the palace roof. Then he climbed through the window of the princess's room. It was quite easy!

She was fast asleep on a sofa, and she looked so beautiful that the merchant's son could not help but give her a kiss. This woke her up. Oh, she was frightened to see a strange young man bending over her. But he explained that he was a Turkish god and had come flying down from the sky to call on her. She liked that story.

Then they sat side by side, and he told her tales about her eyes; they were deep and lovely lakes, he said, and her thoughts swam through them like mermaids. He told her about her forehead; it was a snowy mountain, but inside were wonderful rooms and galleries, with the loveliest pictures on the walls. And he told her about the stork, which flies in with charming little babies — tales of that kind. And then he asked her to marry him, and she said yes.

"But you must come here on Saturday," she said. "That's when my parents, the king and queen, will be having tea with me. They *will* be proud that I am going to marry a Turkish god. But do be sure to tell them some good stories—they'll enjoy that so much. Only, my mother likes tales with a moral, very proper, you know, while Father prefers something lively, to make him laugh."

"Very well," said the merchant's son. "A story shall be my wedding present."

So they parted, but the princess gave him a sword that was decorated with gold coins. He had plenty of use for those.

Off he flew, and he bought himself a new dressing gown. Then he sat down in the woods to think about his story. It had to be ready by Saturday, and that wasn't so easy. But at last it was finished and Saturday had arrived.

The king and queen and all the court were at the tea party, waiting for him to come. They gave him a charming welcome.

"Now, do tell us a story," said the queen. "But mind, it must have a serious moral."

"Yes, yes, but you must make us laugh, as well," said the king.

"I'll do my best," said the young man, and he began his story. "Now, listen carefully. . . .

116

"Once upon a time there was a bundle of matches. They were extremely proud and haughty, because they came from such high beginnings. Their family tree — the one they had all been taken from — had once been a tall and ancient pine tree in the forest. Now the matches lay on a kitchen shelf between a tinderbox and an old iron pot, and they told these neighbors all about the time when they were young.

'Ah yes,' they said, 'we were on top of the world when we were on that tree. Every morning and evening we had diamond tea — they call it dew — and all day we had sunshine (when there *was* any sunshine), and all the little birds had to tell us stories. We could easily see that we were grander than the rest: we could afford green clothes all the year round, while the poor oaks and beeches wore leaves only in summertime.

'But then the woodcutter came — we call it the Great Revolution — and the family was split up. Our mighty trunk found a place as the mainmast of a great ship that could sail around the world if she'd a mind to. Jobs of various kinds were found for the branches, and we were appointed to bring light to the lower orders. You must be wondering how such highborn persons as ourselves came to be in this kitchen. Now you know.'

'I have a different history,' said the iron pot. 'Ever since I first came into the world, I have been scrubbed and boiled, boiled and scrubbed — I can't count the number of times. I do the solid work here, the only kind that matters. Strictly speaking, I'm the number-one person in this house. What do I most enjoy? I'll tell you. It's to settle down on this shelf, clean and tidy, when all the business of dinner is over, and have a sensible chat with friends. Except for the water bucket, which goes into the yard now and then, we all prefer to stay at home. None of that foreign travel for us. The only one who brings in news is the shopping basket. But it's wild, disagreeable stuff, always about the government and the people. Why! Only the other day an elderly jug in this kitchen was so shaken by what the basket said that he fell down and broke into pieces. He was absolutely shattered.

Yes, she's a real troublemaker, that basket; I wouldn't trust her politics at all.'

'You do ramble on,' growled the tinderbox, and it clashed its flint and steel to give out sparks. 'I was hoping for a livelier evening.'

'Yes,' said the matches, 'we do need brightening up. What about discussing which of us comes from the best family? That would be interesting.'

'No, I don't like talking about myself,' said an earthenware pot. 'Let's do something more entertaining. For a start I'll tell you a story, the kind we can all enter into. Right? On the Baltic shores, where the Danish beech trees wave their boughs —'

'What a fine beginning!' said the plates. 'We like this story already.'

'Well,' continued the earthenware pot, 'it was there that I spent my youth, in a very respectable household. The furniture was polished every week, the floors washed every day, and clean curtains were put up every fortnight.'

'You make it all sound so interesting,' said the broom. 'Anyone can tell you're a lady. Your story is so clean and refined.'

'Yes, I thought that, too,' said the water bucket, and it gave a hop and skip of pleasure —*Plink! Plop!*— on the kitchen floor. The pot went on with her story, and the end was just as good as the beginning. The plates all clattered together — that was their way of showing applause — while the broom took some parsley from the dustbin and put it around the pot like a crown; he knew that this would annoy the others. *If I crown her today,* he thought, *she'll crown me tomorrow.*

'Now I'm going to dance,' said the tongs, and dance she did. My, my, how high she could kick her legs! The old chintz chair cover split right down the middle trying to get a good view. 'Where's my crown?' the tongs demanded when the dance was done. So she was crowned as well.

A common, vulgar lot, thought the matches, but they kept the thought to themselves.

The big tea urn was asked to sing, but she had a cold, she said; unless she

118

was on the boil she wasn't in good voice. The truth was that she was too conceited and proud to sing in the kitchen. She would only perform in the dining room, when the master and mistress were present.

Over on the window ledge was an old quill pen that the maidservant used. There was nothing special about her except for the fact that she had been dipped too deep in the inkwell. This seemed to the pen a mark of distinction, and she was quite vain about it. 'If the tea urn doesn't wish to sing,' said the pen, 'why should we try to make her? There's a nightingale outside; she can manage a few notes. It's true that she has never had lessons — the bird is quite uneducated — but let's not be fussy tonight.'

'I don't approve at all,' said the kettle. She was the kitchen's chief vocalist, and also half-sister to the tea urn. 'Why should we listen to a foreign bird? Is it patriotic? I put it to the shopping basket — don't you think I am right?'

'I'm really disappointed,' said the basket. 'Is this the proper way to spend an evening, squabbling and squabbling? Wouldn't it be better to set our house in order? Let us start by putting everyone in his or her proper place. That, of course, will set me at the top; I'll be in charge. You'll see a few changes!'

'Yes, why not?' said the dishes. 'We could do with a little stirring up.'

But at that moment the door opened. It was the maid. Not one of them moved; not one of them made a sound. Yet every single pot in the place was silently telling itself how gifted it really was, how much above the rest in style and quality. *Given the chance,* each thought, *I could have made a real success of the evening.*

The maid picked up the matches and struck them. How they spluttered and blazed! *Now,* they thought, *everyone can see that we are the top people here. No one can shine like us — what brilliance! What a light we throw on dark places!*

And then they were all burned out."

"That was a lovely tale!" said the queen. "I feel as if I had been in the kitchen all the time, especially with those matches. You shall certainly marry our daughter."

"Yes, yes, of course," said the king. "We'll have the wedding on Monday." And he dropped his royal manner when he spoke, since the young man was now one of the family.

Everything was arranged, and on the eve of the wedding the whole city was lit up. Cakes and buns were thrown to be scrambled for; the street urchins hopped about on tiptoe, cheering and whistling through their fingers. It was a glorious occasion. Just to be there was enough to make anyone happy.

I suppose I ought to be doing something too, thought the merchant's son. So he bought rockets and whiz-bangs, every kind of firework you could think of. Then he put them into his trunk and flew up into the air. *Swoosh! Bang!* How those fireworks blazed and thundered! All the Turks were leaping into the air with the wonder of it; their slippers were flying about their ears. Never in their lives had they seen such a fantastic show. Now they were certain that the princess was marrying a real Turkish god.

When the merchant's son reached the woods, he thought he would go back to the town to hear

for himself what the people were saying about his fiery flight. You might have done the same yourself — it was perfectly natural. Goodness, how they were talking! Every person had a different version of the happening, but they all thought it magical.

"I saw the Turkish god himself," said one. "He had eyes like glittering stars and a beard like the rolling waves!"

"He wore a great cloak of fire," said another. "I saw cherubs peeping from the folds — lovely little things, they were."

Oh, yes, there was plenty of good listening for the young man. And the next day was to be his wedding day.

At last he went back to the woods to get his trunk — but what had become of it? The trunk was burned to cinders. A spark from the fireworks had set it alight, and all that remained was ashes. He could not fly, so he could not get back to his bride.

All day she stood waiting on the roof. She is waiting still. As for him, he goes wandering around the world, on foot, telling fairy tales. But somehow none is as lighthearted as the one he told of the matches. ᵔ

The Ugly Duckling

*T*he despised and misunderstood outsider on a harsh and lonely
path, almost beyond hope, meeting at last a shining triumph,
is the basis of fairy lore, and at some time everyone's daydream.
But for Andersen it was truth. This was his autobiography.

The idea came to him in July 1842 when he was staying at
Gisselfeldt, one of the great manor houses of the Danish aristocracy.
Wandering the grounds in a downcast mood, he stopped to
watch the swans on the lake. His gloom disappeared. Three weeks
later, as guest of another manor, he noted down, "Began 'The Cygnet'
yesterday." But it was more than a year before "The Cygnet" was done
to his liking — many revisions, much rewording. In October 1843
he wrote at last, "Finished the tale of the young swan."

It is a superb piece of writing — even in English translation.
The Andersen use of detail is at its most relevant and perceptive:
as the seasons change, the Danish landscape reflects the sad bird's
fortunes as he seeks a friend, seeks shelter. This could be the most
moving of all the great early Andersen stories. Yet, at the same time,
the one most lightened by Andersen's straight-faced humor, especially
evident in the overheard farmyard chatter and other verbal exchanges.

As a reader-aloud of his own work, Andersen was unsurpassed,
and this tale was always a favorite.

*J*T WAS SO DELIGHTFUL IN THE COUNTRY. The air was full of summer, the corn was yellow, the oats were ripe, the haystacks in the meadows looked like little hills of grass, and there the stork strutted about on his long, red legs. All around the open fields were woods and forests, and within these were deep, cool lakes. Yes, it really was delightful in the countryside. And there, in the bright sunshine, stood an old manor house surrounded by a moat. Great dock leaves grew from the wall as far down as the water — some of them so big that little children could stand upright underneath them. In their shade, you might think yourself in a tiny secret forest of your own.

This was where a duck sat on her nest and waited for her ducklings to hatch. She was becoming rather tired of sitting there, though, for the ducklings took so long to come; as for visitors, she hardly ever had any —

 the other ducks preferred swimming in the moat to dropping in under the dock leaves for a chat.

But at last the eggs began to crack, one after another. "Peep, peep!" The nest was full of little birds poking their heads from the shell.

"Quack, quack!" said the mother. "Quick, quick!" So the little things came out as fast as they could, and stared all around their leafy green shelter; and their mother let them look as much as they liked, for green is good for the eyes.

"How big the world is!" the young ones said. And certainly they had much more space now than they'd had inside the eggs.

"Do you suppose that this is all the world, you foolish little creatures?" said their mother. "Why — the world stretches out far beyond the other side of the garden, right into the parson's field. Though, to be sure, I have never been there myself. You *are* all here now, aren't you?" She got up from the nest. "No, you're not. There's still the biggest egg. How much longer is it going to be? I'm really tired of this business, I can tell you." And down she sat again.

"Well, how are things going?" asked an old duck who had come to pay a call.

"This egg is taking a dreadfully long time," said the mother duck. "It just won't hatch! But do look at the others; they are the prettiest little ducklings I have ever seen, the living image of their father, too — that wretch, who never comes to visit me!"

"Let me look at the egg," said the old duck. "Ah! Take my word for it, that's a turkey's egg. I was once played the same trick, and the trouble I had with the young ones! Being turkeys, they were afraid of the water, and I *couldn't* get them to go in. I quacked and scolded, but it was no use. Let me see. Yes, that's a turkey's egg. Just let it be, and go off and teach the rest to swim."

"Well, I'll sit on it a bit longer," said the duck. "As I have sat so long, I may as well finish off the job."

"Oh, well, please yourself," said the old duck, and she went away.

At last the big egg cracked. "Peep, peep!" said the young one as he tumbled out. But how big and ugly he was! The mother looked at him. *That's a terribly big duckling,* she thought. *Can he be a turkey chick, after*

*all? Well, we shall soon find out; into the water he shall go, even if
I have to push him in myself.*

The next day the weather was beautiful, and the mother duck came
out with all her young ones and went down to the moat. *Splash!* In she
went. "Quack, quack!" she called, and one after another the ducklings
plopped in. The water went over their heads, but they rose up again in a
moment and were soon swimming busily. Their feet moved of their own
accord, and there they all were, out in the water — even the ugly gray one
was swimming with them.

"No, that's no turkey,"
the mother said. "Look how
well he uses his legs, and
how straight he holds himself. He's my own child, no
doubt about it. Really, he is
quite handsome if you look
at him properly. Quack,
quack! Come along with

me, children; I'll take you into the world and introduce you to the other
farm birds; but mind you stay close to me, so that no one treads on you.
And keep a careful lookout for the cat."

So they went into the poultry yard. There was a horrible noise and
commotion there, for two families were squabbling over the head of an
eel — and then the cat got it, after all.

"That's the way of the world," said the mother duck. Her own beak
watered a little, for she, too, would have liked the eel's head. "Now then,
use your legs — hurry along and make a bow to the old duck over there!
She is our most distinguished resident; her ancestors came from Spain,

and, as you can see, she has a piece of red cloth tied around her leg. That is something very special; it means that no one will get rid of her, and both man and beast must treat her with respect. Come along! Don't turn your toes in! A well-bred duckling walks with feet well apart, like Father and Mother. Now then! Make a bow and say, 'Quack!'"

The little birds did as they were told, but the other ducks in the yard looked at them and said quite loudly, "Now we shall have to put up with all that mob, as if there weren't enough of us already. And — my goodness! What an odd-looking duckling that one is! We certainly don't want him!" And a duck flew at the gray one and pecked him in the neck.

"Leave him alone," said the mother. "He's not doing anyone any harm."

"Yes, but he's too big, and peculiar-looking," said the duck who had pecked at him. "He has to be put in his place."

"There's a fine family," said the old duck with the piece of red cloth around her leg. "All the children are pretty — except *that* one; he won't do at all. I do wish that the mother could make him all over again."

"That can't be done, your grace," said the mother duck. "To be sure, he isn't handsome, but he has a nice disposition, and he swims quite as prettily as any of the others. I venture to say, he may even grow to be better-looking, and perhaps, in time, a bit smaller. He has lain too long in the egg, and that has spoiled his shape." And she tidied the fluff on the back of his neck and smoothed him down here and there. "Besides," she said, "he's a drake, so it doesn't matter quite as much about looks. He is healthy, I'm sure, and he'll make his way in the world well enough."

"Anyhow, the other ducklings are charming," said the old duck. "Well, make yourselves at home—and if you happen to come across an eel's head, you can bring it to me."

That was only the first day; after that, the gray one's plight grew worse. How wretched he felt to be so ugly! He was chased about by everyone. The ducks snapped at him, the hens, too, and the girl who came to feed them shoved him with her foot. Even his brothers and sisters were against him, and kept saying, "You ugly thing! We hope the cat gets you!" His mother, too, would murmur, "I wish you were far away."

So away he went. First, he flew over the fence—and the little birds in the bushes rose up into the air with alarm. *That's because I am so ugly,* the duckling thought, and shut his eyes. But he went on all the same. At last, he reached the wide marshes where the wild ducks lived, and he lay there all the night, for he was so tired and sad.

In the morning the wild ducks flew up and considered their new companion. "What kind of creature are you?" they asked, and the duckling turned from one to another and greeted them as politely as he could.

"You're certainly ugly, that's a fact!" said a wild duck. "Still, that doesn't matter so long as you don't marry into the family."

Poor little outcast! The idea of marriage had never even entered his head. All he wanted was to lie and rest in the reeds, and to have a drink of marsh water.

There he lay for two whole days; then he was visited by

a pair of wild geese — young ganders, really, for both were male birds. They were only recently hatched, and were as lively and saucy as could be. "Listen, friend," they said. "You're so ugly that we rather like you. What about coming with us when we fly farther afield? In another marsh not far from here there are some charming young wild geese, lovely girls, whose 'Quack!' is worth hearing. With your funny looks, you might be quite a success with them."

At that moment there was a *Bang! Bang!* and both the happy-go-lucky young ganders fell down dead in the reeds. The water became quite red with blood. Again, *Bang! Bang!* — and a great flock of wild geese flew up from the rushes. A big shoot was going on. The sportsmen were stationed all round the marsh; some were even in the trees overhanging the reeds. Blue smoke drifted like clouds in and out of the dark branches and floated over the water. The dogs went *Splash! Splash!* through the mud, treading down the rushes. The poor duckling was terrified; just as he was trying to hide his head under his wing, a huge and frightful dog stood before him, tongue hanging out of his mouth and eyes gleaming horribly. He thrust his muzzle at the duckling,  showed his sharp teeth, and then — *splash!* He was off without touching the bird.

"Oh, thank goodness," said the duckling. "I'm so ugly that even the dog thinks twice before biting me." And he lay quite still while shot after shot whined and banged through the reeds.

The day was far on before the noise stopped, but the poor young thing dared not move even then. At last, however, he lifted up his head, peered cautiously around, then hurried away from the marsh as fast as he could. Over fields and meadows he ran, while the wind blew so harshly against him that it was hard work to get along.

Toward evening he reached a miserable hovel, which was in such a crazy state by now that it couldn't decide which way to tumble down, so it remained standing. The wind howled so fiercely around the duckling that he had to sit down on his tail to avoid being blown over — and the wind grew fiercer still. Then he noticed that the door had lost a hinge and was hanging so crookedly that he could slip through the crack, and that is what he did.

In the hovel lived an old woman with a cat and a hen. The cat, whom she called Sonny, could arch his back and purr; he could give out sparks, too, but only when he was stroked the wrong way. The hen had little short legs, and so was called Chicky Short-Legs. She laid well, and the old woman was as fond of her as if she were her own child.

When morning came, the strange little visitor was noticed at once: the cat began to purr and the hen to cluck. "What's the matter?" said the old woman, looking all about her. But her sight was none too good, so she

mistook the little newcomer for a full-grown bird. "Here's a piece of luck, and no mistake," said she. "Now I can have duck eggs — as long as it isn't a drake. Well, we shall see." And the duckling was taken in on approval for three weeks; but no eggs appeared.

The cat was the master of the house and the hen the mistress; they were always saying, "We and the world," for they looked on themselves as half the world, and the better half at that. The duckling thought that there might be other opinions on that matter, but the hen would not hear of it.

"Can you lay eggs?" she asked. "No? Then kindly keep your views to yourself!"

The cat asked, "Can you arch your back and purr, or give out sparks? No? Then you had better keep quiet while sensible people are talking."

So the duckling sat in a corner and moped. Thoughts of fresh air and sunshine came into his mind, and then an extraordinary longing seized him to float on the water. At last he could not help telling the hen about it.

"What a preposterous notion!" she exclaimed. "The trouble with you is that you have nothing to do; that's why you get these fancies. Just lay a few eggs, or practice purring, and they'll pass."

"But it is so delicious to float on the water," said the duckling. "It is so lovely to put down your head and dive to the bottom."

"That *must* be delightful!" said the hen sarcastically. "You must be out of your mind! Ask the cat — he's the cleverest person I know — if he likes floating on the water or diving to the bottom. Never mind my opinion: ask our mistress, the old woman; there's no one wiser in the whole world. Do you imagine that *she* wants to float or put her head underwater?"

"You don't understand," said the duckling sadly.

"Well, if we don't understand you, nobody will. You'll never be as wise as the cat and the old woman, to say nothing of myself. Don't give yourself airs, child, but be thankful for all the good things that have been done for you. Haven't you found a warm room and elegant company, from whom you can learn plenty if you listen? But all you do is talk nonsense; you're not even cheerful to be with. Believe me, I mean this for your own good. Now do make an effort to lay some eggs, or at least learn to purr and give out sparks."

"I think I had better go out into the wide world," said the duckling.

"All right, do," said the hen.

So the duckling went. He floated on the water, and he dived below the surface; but it seemed to him that other ducks ignored him because of his ugliness.

Now autumn came: the leaves in the woods turned brown and yellow, and the wind caught them and whirled them madly around; the very sky looked chill; the clouds hung heavy with hail and snow; and the raven, perched on the fence, cried, "Caw! Caw!" because of the cold. Even to look at the scene was enough to make you shiver. It was a hard time for the duckling, too.

One evening, as the sky flamed with the setting sun, a flock of marvelous great birds rose out of the rushes. The duckling had never seen any birds so beautiful. They were brilliantly white, with long, graceful necks — indeed, they were swans; uttering a strange sound, they spread their splendid wings and flew far away to warmer lands and lakes that did not freeze. High in the air they soared, and the ugly duckling was filled with a wild excitement; he turned around and around in the water like a wheel, and called out in a voice so loud and strange that it quite frightened him. Oh, he would never forget those wonderful birds, those fortunate birds! As soon as the last was out of sight, he dived right down to the bottom of the water, and when he came up again, he was almost frantic. He did not know what the birds were called; he did not know where they had come from, nor where they were flying — but he felt more deeply drawn to them than to anything he had ever known.

The winter grew colder still. The duckling had to swim around and around in the water to keep it from freezing over, but every night the ice-free part became smaller. Then he had to use his feet all the time to break up the surface; at last, however, he was quite worn out. He lay still and was frozen fast in the ice.

Early next morning, a peasant came by. Seeing the bird, he went out, broke up the ice with his wooden clogs, and carried him home to his wife. Presently the duckling came to life again. The children wanted to play with him, but he thought that they meant to hurt him, and in his fright he flew into the milk pail. The milk splashed all over the room and the woman shrieked and threw up her hands—then he flew into the butter tub, then into the flour barrel, and out again. Goodness, what a sight he was! The woman, still screaming, hit out at him with the fire tongs; the children, laughing and shrieking, tumbled over one another as they tried to grab the little creature. Luckily, the door stood open; out he rushed into the bushes and the new-fallen snow, and there he lay in a kind of swoon.

But it would be too sad to tell you of all the hardships and miseries that he had to go through during that cruel winter. One day he was huddling among the reeds in the marsh when the sun began to send down warm rays again; the larks started their song; how glorious! It was spring. The duckling raised his wings. They seemed stronger than before, and carried him swiftly away. Before he realized what was happening, he was in a lovely garden full of apple trees in blossom, and where sweet-smelling lilac hung on its long boughs right down to the winding stream. And then, directly in front of him, out of the leafy shadows, came three magnificent white swans, ruffling their feathers as they floated lightly over the water. The duckling recognized the wonderful birds, and a strange sadness came over him.

"I will fly to those noble birds, even though they may peck me to death for daring to come near them, an ugly thing like me. But I don't care— better be killed by such splendid creatures than be pecked by ducks and hens and kicked by the poultry-yard girl, or be left to suffer another winter like the last." So he flew out to the open water and swam toward the glorious swans. They saw him and came speeding toward him, ruffling their plumage.

"Yes, kill me," said the poor creature, bowing his head right down to the water as he waited for his end. Yet what did he see reflected below?

He beheld his own likeness — but he was no longer an awkward, ugly, dark, gray bird. He was like the proud white birds about him; he was a swan.

It doesn't matter if you are born in a duck yard, so long as you come from a swan's egg.

He felt glad that he had suffered so much hardship and trouble, for now he could value his good fortune and the home he had found at last. The stately swans swam around him and stroked him admiringly with their beaks. Some little children came into the garden and threw bread into the water, and the smallest of all cried joyfully, "There's a new one!" And the others called out in delight, "Yes, a new swan has come!" They clapped their hands and danced about with pleasure. Then they ran to tell their father and mother. More bread and cake were thrown into the water, and everyone said, "The new one is the most beautiful of all. Look how handsome he is, that young one there." And the older swans bowed before him.

He felt quite shy, and hid his head under his wing; he did not know what to do. He was almost too happy, yet he was not proud, for a good heart is never proud or vain. He remembered the time when he had been persecuted and scorned, yet now he heard everyone saying that he was the most beautiful of all these beautiful birds. The lilacs bowed their branches down to the water to greet him, the sun sent down its friendly warmth, and the young bird, his heart filled with joy, ruffled his feathers, raised his slender neck, and said, "I never dreamed that such happiness could ever be when I was the ugly duckling.

On October 13, 1843, Andersen noted in his diary: "Began the Chinese tale." A month later it was published. Why Chinese? A childhood memory in his autobiography gives the clue:

"An old woman rinsing out clothes in the Odense River told me that the Empire of China lay directly underneath. I did not think it impossible that a Chinese prince, on some moonlit night, might dig himself up through the earth; hearing me sing he would take me down to his kingdom, make me rich and noble, and then let me return to Odense. There I would . . . build myself a castle. I spent many evenings working out the plan for this."

"The Nightingale" is an extraordinary story. As it opens, we are in a sheer lighthearted, magical fairy tale — in a palace almost beyond imagining. Yet after an episode or so of hilarious comedy, we move into one of the most haunting passages in the whole of Andersen's work: the great finale, in which Death comes for the emperor. But so, too, does a bargainer for his life — the long-banished nightingale.

Y OU KNOW, OF COURSE, THAT IN CHINA THE EMPEROR is Chinese and that all the people around him are Chinese, too. This story happened many years ago, but that is exactly why you should hear it now, before it is forgotten.

The emperor's palace was the finest in the world, made entirely of the rarest porcelain — absolutely beyond price, but so fragile and delicate that you had to take the greatest care when you moved about. The palace garden was full of marvelous flowers never seen anywhere else; the loveliest of all had little silver bells tied to them — *tinkle, tinkle* — to make sure that nobody passed without noticing.

Yes, everything in the emperor's garden was wonderfully planned, and it stretched so far that even the gardener had no idea where it ended. If you kept on walking, you would find yourself in a most beautiful forest with towering trees and very deep lakes. This forest went right down to the sea, which was blue and deep; great ships could sail right in under the high branches of the trees. In these branches lived a nightingale, which sang so sweetly that even the poor fisherman, with all his cares, would stop while casting his nets each night to listen. "Ah, it's a treat to hear it," he would say. But then he would have to get on with his work

and so would forget the bird. Yet the following night, as soon as the nightingale sang again, the fisherman would look up from his nets and say once more, "Ah, it's a treat to hear it."

From every country in the world travelers came to admire the emperor's city, his palace, and his garden. But as soon as they heard the nightingale, they would all declare, "Now *that's* the best thing of all!" And when they were back at home, these travelers would go on talking about the bird. Learned men wrote books about the city and the palace and the garden, but the nightingale was praised above all other marvels, and poets wrote thrilling poems about the bird in the forest near the sea.

These books were read all over the world, and one day some of them reached the emperor, too. There he sat in his golden chair, reading and reading; now and then he nodded his head. He was pleased to see such splendid descriptions of his realm. Then he came to this sentence: "But, with all these wonders, nothing can match the nightingale."

"What's this!" said the emperor. "The nightingale? Why, I've never heard of it. Just imagine! The things one can learn from books!"

So he sent for his lord-in-waiting. "I see in this book that we have a most remarkable bird called a nightingale," said the emperor. "It is supposed to be the finest thing in my vast empire. Why has no one ever told me about it?"

"Well," said the lord-in-waiting, "I have never heard anyone mention the creature. Certainly it has never been presented at court."

"It is my wish that it comes here tonight and sings to me," said the emperor. "It's a disgrace that the whole world knows what I possess — and I don't."

"I have never heard it mentioned," repeated the lord-in-waiting. "But I'll look for it — I'll find it."

Yes, but where? The lord-in-waiting ran up and down all the stairs, through all the halls and passages, but of all the people he met, not one had ever heard of the nightingale. So he hurried back to the emperor and said that it must be a tale invented by the writers of those books. "Your imperial majesty must not believe all that appears in print. The things these authors invent! It's a real black art!"

"But the book in which I learned about the bird," said the emperor, "was sent to me by the high and mighty emperor of Japan, so it cannot be untrue. I *will* hear the nightingale! I'm determined to hear it tonight."

"*Tsing-pe!*" said the lord-in-waiting, and once more he ran up and down all the staircases and through all the halls and passages; half the court ran with him.

At last they came across a poor little girl in the kitchen. "The nightingale?" she said. "My goodness, yes, of course I know it. How that

bird can sing! Most evenings, after work, they let me take home a few leftover scraps for my sick mother; she lives by the lake at the other side of the forest. And when I am on my way back and feeling tired, I sit down for a while and listen. Then I hear the nightingale."

"Little kitchen-maid!" said the lord-in-waiting. "I shall guarantee you a permanent kitchen appointment and permission to watch the emperor dining, if only you will lead us to the nightingale. Its presence is commanded at court this very evening."

So they set out for the forest where the nightingale usually sang, and nearly half the court joined in the expedition. As they trailed along, a cow began to moo.

"Oh!" exclaimed a court page. "Now we can hear it! For such a small creature it makes an extraordinarily powerful noise. But—do you know—I'm sure I have heard it before."

"No, no, that's a cow mooing," said the little kitchen-maid. "We've still a long way to go."

Some frogs began croaking in the pond. "Glorious!" said the emperor's chaplain. "Now I hear the song! It's just like tiny church bells!"

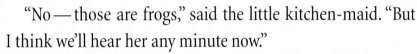

"No—those are frogs," said the little kitchen-maid. "But I think we'll hear her any minute now."

Then the nightingale began to sing. "There she is," said the girl. "Listen! Look!—There she sits." And she pointed to a little gray bird up among the branches.

"Is it possible?" said the lord-in-waiting. "I would never have thought it. How ordinary the creature looks! How plain! Perhaps it has lost its color at the sight of all these distinguished visitors."

"Little nightingale!" the kitchen-maid called. "Our gracious emperor would very much like you to sing for him."

"With the greatest of pleasure," said the nightingale, and she sang so beautifully that it was a delight to hear.

"It sounds just like glass bells," said the lord-in-waiting. "I can't imagine why we have never heard it before. It will be a great hit at court!"

"Shall I sing once again for the emperor?" said the nightingale, for she thought that the emperor was one of these visitors.

"Most excellent nightingale," said the lord-in-waiting, "I have the honor and pleasure to summon you to a concert this evening at the palace, where you will enchant his imperial majesty with your delightful song."

"It sounds best out in the green forest," said the nightingale. Still, she went along willingly enough when she heard that the emperor wished it.

Meanwhile, what a cleaning and polishing was going on at the palace! The porcelain walls and floor gleamed and sparkled in the light of thousands of golden lamps. Right in the middle of the great hall, where the emperor sat, a golden perch was set up; this was for the nightingale. Everyone in the court was there; the little kitchen-maid was allowed to stand behind the door, for now she had the official title of Genuine Maid of

the Kitchen. All eyes were turned on the little gray bird as the emperor nodded at her to begin.

Then the nightingale sang so beautifully that tears came to the emperor's eyes and rolled right down his cheeks, and she sang on even more thrillingly, so that every note went straight to his heart. The emperor was greatly pleased — the nightingale, he declared, should have his golden slipper to wear around her neck.

But she thanked him and refused, for she had already had her reward. "I have

seen tears in the emperor's eyes — can any gift be greater than that? An emperor's tears have a strange power. I have had pay enough." And then she sang yet another song in her ravishing voice.

"Very saucy, very amusing; the creature is quite a flirt," said the court ladies, and they filled their mouths with water to make a gurgling sound. Why shouldn't they be nightingales, too? Even the lackeys and chambermaids nodded their approval, and that means a great deal,

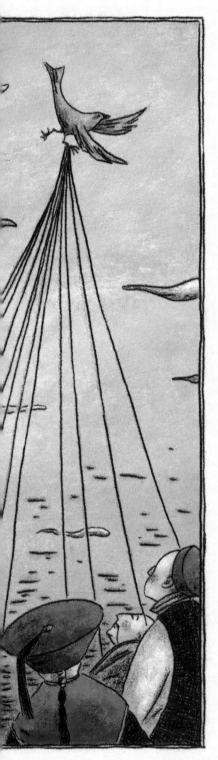

for they are the hardest of all to satisfy. There was no doubt about it — the nightingale really was a hit.

From now on she was to remain at court and have her own cage, with permission to take to the air twice in the daytime and once each night. With her on each excursion went twelve attendants, each one holding on firmly to a silk ribbon tied to the bird's leg. No, there was not much fun in these outings. One day a large parcel arrived for the emperor. On it was written one word:

NIGHTINGALE

"Why, here's a new book about our famous bird!" said the emperor. But it was not a book; it was a little mechanical toy in a box, a clockwork nightingale. It was made to look like the real one, but it was covered all over with diamonds, rubies, and sapphires. If you wound it up, it would sing one of the songs that the real bird sang, and its tail would go up and down, glittering with silver and gold. Around its neck hung a ribbon on which was written, "The emperor of Japan's nightingale is a poor thing beside the nightingale of the emperor of China."

"How delightful!" everyone said. And the messenger who had brought the bird was given the title of Chief Imperial Bringer of Nightingales. "Now they must sing together — what a duet that will be!"

So the two birds sang together, but it was not a success. The trouble was that the real nightingale sang in her own way, and the other bird's song came out of a machine. "There's nothing to be ashamed of in that," said the Master of the Imperial Music. "It keeps excellent time — in fact, it could be one of my own pupils."

So the clockwork bird was set to sing alone. It pleased the court quite as much as the real one, and of course it was a great deal prettier to look at, glittering there like a bracelet or a brooch. Over and over, thirty-three times, it sang the same tune, and yet it was not in the least tired. The courtiers would gladly have heard it a few times more, but now the emperor thought that the real one should have a turn.

Only where *was* the nightingale? She had flown out the open window, away to her own green forest, and no one had noticed.

"Tut, tut, tut!" said the emperor. "What's the meaning of this?" And the courtiers muttered and frowned. "Still, we have the better bird here," they added, and the clockwork bird had to sing its song again. That was the thirty-fourth time they had heard it, but they weren't quite sure of it even yet. It was a difficult tune to learn. And the Master of the Imperial Music praised the bird in the highest terms; it was superior to the living nightingale not only in its outward appearance — all those sparkling jewels — but in its internal workings, too. "You see, ladies and gentlemen, and above all your imperial majesty, with the real nightingale, you can never tell what will happen, but with the clockwork bird, you can be certain; everything is clear; you can open it and see how the thoughts are arranged, how each note must precisely follow the one before."

"Why, that's just what I was thinking," each one agreed. And the following Sunday, the Master of the Imperial Music was allowed to give a public display of the bird to the ordinary people. They, too, must hear it sing, the emperor declared. And hear it they did, and they were

as intoxicated by it as if they had made themselves tipsy on tea, an ancient Chinese custom. They all said "Ah!" and held up their forefingers in the air and nodded their heads.

But the poor fisherman who had heard the real nightingale said, "It's pretty enough—sounds quite like the bird, too. Yet there's something kind of missing. I don't know what."

The real nightingale was banished from the emperor's realm.

The artificial bird was awarded a special place on a silk cushion close to the emperor's bed; piled around were all the gifts it had been given, all the gold and jewels. It was honored with the title of High Imperial Minstrel of the Bedside Table, Class One on the Left, for even an emperor keeps his heart on the left. The Master of the Imperial Music wrote a solemn work in twenty-five volumes about the mechanical bird. It was extremely long and learned, full of the most difficult Chinese words. But everyone pretended to have read it and to have understood it, too. Nobody wished to be thought stupid!

All this went on for a whole year, until the emperor, his court, and the rest of the Chinese people all knew by heart every little trill and cluck in the toy bird's song, but for that very reason they liked it all the more. They could join in the song themselves, and this they did. The street boys went about singing, "*Zirril, zirril, kluk, kluk, kluk,*" and the emperor sang it, too —a delightful noise, no doubt about that.

But one evening, just as the clockwork bird was singing away and the emperor was lying in bed listening to it, something went *snap!* inside the bird. *Whirr-rr-rr!* The wheels went whizzing around and the music stopped. The emperor leaped out of bed and sent for his own doctor. But what was the use of that? So they went and fetched the watchmaker, and after a lot of muttering and poking about, he managed to patch up the

bird after a fashion. But he warned them that it would have to be used very sparingly; the bearings were almost worn away, and it would be impossible to replace them without ruining the sound.

What a dreadful blow! They dared not let the bird sing more than once a year, and even that was taking a risk. However, on these annual occasions, the Master of the Imperial Music would make a speech full of difficult words, saying that the bird was just as good as ever — and so, of course, since he said so, it was just as good as ever.

Five years passed, and a great sorrow fell upon the land. The people were very fond of their emperor, but now he was gravely ill and was not expected to live. A new emperor had already been chosen, and crowds stood outside in the street and asked the lord-in-waiting for news. How was the emperor? The lord-in-waiting shook his head.

Cold and pale, the emperor lay in his royal bed. Indeed, the whole court now believed him gone, and went running off to greet his successor. The servants of the bedchamber ran out to gossip; the palace maids held a big coffee party. In all the halls and corridors, black cloth had been laid down to dull the sound of footsteps, so the whole palace seemed very, very still.

But the emperor was not yet dead. Pale and unmoving, he lay in his magnificent bed with its long velvet curtains and heavy tassels of gold. Through a high open window, the moon shone down on the emperor and the artificial bird.

The poor emperor could hardly breathe; he felt as if something were sitting on his heart. He opened his eyes and saw that Death was seated there. Death was wearing the emperor's golden crown; in one hand he held the Imperial golden sword, in the other the splendid Imperial banner. And out of the folds of the great velvet curtains, strange faces

pushed and peeped; some were hideous, others lovely and kind. They were the emperor's evil and good deeds, looking back at him, as Death sat on his heart.

"Do you remember . . . ? Do you remember . . . ?" came the rustling whispers, one after another. And they told and recalled so many things that sweat at last broke out on the emperor's forehead.

"I never knew — I never realized," he cried. "Music — music! Beat the great drum of China! Save me from those voices!"

But the voices did not stop. On and on they went, while Death nodded like a mandarin at everything that was said.

"Music! Let me have music!" begged the emperor. "Beautiful little

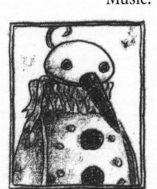

golden bird, sing — I ask you, sing! I have given you gold and precious things; I hung my golden slipper about your neck with my own hands. Sing! I beseech you — sing!"

But the bird was silent; there was no one to wind it up, and unless it was wound, it had no voice. And Death went on gazing at the emperor out of his great empty eye sockets. Everything was still, terribly still.

Then, all at once, close by the window, the loveliest song rang out. It came from the living nightingale, who had flown to a branch outside. Hearing of the emperor's need, the little bird had returned to bring him comfort and hope.

As she sang, the ghostly forms grew more and more shadowy, until they thinned away into nothing. The blood began to flow faster through the emperor's body. Death himself was held by the song. "Sing more — sing more, little nightingale," said Death.

"Yes, if you will give me the great gold sword. . . . Yes, if you will give me the rich banner. . . . Yes, if you will give me the emperor's crown."

So Death gave up each of the treasures in return for a song, and the nightingale went on singing. She sang of the quiet churchyard where the white roses grow, where the elderflowers smell so sweet, where the fresh grass is kept green by the tears of those who mourn. Then Death was filled with a great longing for his garden, and he floated out of the window like a cold white mist.

"Thank you, thank you," said the emperor. "You heavenly little bird, I know who you are. I banished you from my realm, and yet you alone came to my need, and drove the dreadful phantoms from my bed, and freed my heart from Death. How can I reward you?"

"You have rewarded me," said the nightingale. "When I first sang to you, tears came to your eyes, and that gift I cannot forget. These are the jewels that cannot be bought or sold. But now you must sleep and grow well and strong. Listen, I will sing to you."

And she sang, and the emperor fell into a sweet, refreshing sleep.

The sun was shining on him through the window when he woke, restored — all his illness, all his weakness gone. None of his servants had yet looked in; they all thought he was dead. But the nightingale was still there, singing.

"You must stay with me always," said the emperor. "You need sing only when you wish. And as for the clockwork bird, I'll break that into a thousand pieces."

"Don't do that," said the nightingale. "It has done what it could for you. Keep it as you did before. I cannot make my home in a palace, but let me come and go as I wish, and then, in the evenings, I'll sit outside on that branch by the window and sing for you. I shall bring you happiness, but also serious thoughts. I shall sing about those in your realm who are joyful and those who are sad. I shall sing of the good and evil that are all around yet have always been hidden from you. The little bird flies far and wide, to the poor fisherman, to the laborer's cottage, to so many who are far removed from you and your splendid court. I love your heart more than your crown—and yet the crown has some magic about it. Yes, I will come—but one thing you must promise."

"Anything!" said the emperor. He had risen and put on his Imperial robes, and he was holding the heavy golden sword against his heart.

"The one thing I ask of you is this. Tell no one that you have for a friend a little bird who tells you everything. It is best to keep it a secret."

And with that, the nightingale flew away.

The servants came in to see their dead master. Well—there they stood!

"Good morning," said the emperor.

The Snow Queen

"The Snow Queen" is surely Andersen's masterpiece, and certainly the greatest of all invented fairy tales. Yet, unusually, almost nothing is written of its making in Andersen's diaries and letters—with the exception of these words to a friend: "It has been a sheer joy to me to put on paper my new fairy tale 'The Snow Queen.' It took hold of my mind in such a way that it came dancing over the paper." This explains, perhaps, a hardly credible miracle of speed, for it was begun on December 5, 1844, and in print on December 21.

What gives the tale its immense importance in fairy lore is the creation of the Snow Queen herself, that supreme enchantress, of dazzling beauty and awesome powers, neither evil nor good, not borrowed from tale or legend, not ever to be overcome or destroyed. When she is taking the boy Kay to her palace, north of north (the most brilliant passage in all of Andersen's writing) she is Experience. Elsewhere she is the beauty and cruelty of Winter.

For anyone first reading "The Snow Queen" as a child, what stays in the mind? The dreams on the stairs? The robber girl with a dry good sense, setting out—for where? Any one of the four seasons? For my part, it must be the pieces of ice in the freezing palace. They come to mind whenever I have a problem—will I fit the ice shapes into place? And the word they form—why did Andersen choose Eternity? My guess is that it was a sudden inspiration. The "washerwoman's crazy son" was to achieve the peak of fame. Would it last beyond his lifetime? The ice pieces give the answer.

153

Part the First
Which Tells of the Looking Glass and the Splinters

Listen, now! We're going to begin our story. When we come to the end of it, we shall know more than we do now. There was once a wicked imp, a demon, one of the very worst—he was the Devil himself. One day, there he was, laughing his head off. Why? Because he had made a magic mirror with a special power: everything good and beautiful that was reflected in it shriveled up almost to nothing, but everything evil and ugly seemed even larger and more hideous than it was. In this glass, the loveliest landscapes looked just like boiled spinach, and even the nicest people appeared quite horrible, or seemed to be standing on their heads or to have no trunks to their bodies. As for their faces, they were so twisted and changed that no one could have recognized them, and, if anything holy and serious passed through someone's mind, a hideous, sneering grin was shown in the glass. This was a huge joke.

All the students who attended his demon school went around declaring that he'd achieved a miracle; now for the first time everyone could see what the world and its humans were really like. They took the mirror and ran around to the four corners of the earth, until there wasn't a place or person unharmed by the glass.

At last they fixed on a still more daring plan—to fly up to heaven, to make fun of the angels and of God himself. The higher they flew with the mirror, the more it grimaced and twisted; they could scarcely hold on to it. Up and up they went, nearer and nearer to heaven's kingdom — until, disaster! The mirror shook so violently with its weird reflections that it sprang out of their hands and went crashing down to Earth, where it burst into hundreds of millions, billions, trillions of tiny pieces. And that made matters even worse than before, for some of these pieces were hardly as big as a grain of sand. These flew here and there, all through the wide world; whoever got a speck in his eye saw everything good as bad or twisted — for every little splinter had the same power as the whole glass had. Some people even caught a splinter in their hearts, and that was horrible, for then their hearts became just like lumps of ice. Some of the pieces were so big that they were used as windowpanes — but it didn't do to look at your friends through them. Other pieces were made into spectacles — imagine! The demon laughed till he nearly split his sides.

And, as we tell this story, little splinters of magic glass are still flying about in the air. Listen! You shall hear what happened to some of them.

PART THE SECOND
A LITTLE BOY
AND A LITTLE GIRL

*I*n a big city, where there are so many houses and people that there isn't room for everyone to have a garden, and so most people have to make do with flowers in pots, in such a place lived two poor children.

But these two did have a garden a little larger than a flowerpot. They were not brother and sister, but they were just as fond of each other as if they had been. Their parents were next-door neighbors; they lived in attics at the tops of next-door houses. Where the sloping roofs almost touched, a gutter ran along between, and across this, each house had a little window facing the other. You had only to step along the strip of roof to cross from window to window.

The parents each had a wooden box standing outside the window, and here they grew vegetables and herbs. They had little rose trees, too, one in each box, and these grew gloriously. The pea plants trailed over the edges; the rose trees put out long branches, some twining around the windows, some bending over toward the opposite bush, making a kind of arch of leaves and flowers. The children would often sit on their little wooden stools under the roof of roses, and talk and play and spend many a happy hour.

In the winter, of course, there was no sitting out on the roof. The windows were often thick with frost, but the two children would each warm up a coin on the stove, then press it on the frozen pane; this would make a splendid peephole. Behind each round hole was a bright and friendly eye, one at each window. These were the eyes of the little boy and the little girl; his name was Kay and hers was Gerda. In summer they could be together with a single jump, but in winter they had first to climb all the way down one set of stairs, then up another — while outside the snow fell fast.

"Those are the white bees swarming," said the old grandmother.

"Have they a queen, too?" asked the little boy, for he knew that real bees did.

"Yes, indeed," said the grandmother. "Wherever the flakes swarm most thickly, there she flies; she is the largest of them all. She never lies still on the ground, though, but soars up once again into the black cloud. On many a winter night she'll fly through the streets of the town and peer in at the windows, and then they freeze into the strangest patterns, like stars and flowers."

"Yes, I've seen that!" both children cried at once, knowing now that it must be true.

"Could the Snow Queen come in here?" asked the little girl.

"Just let her try!" said the boy. "I'll put her on the hot stove, and then she'll melt."

But the grandmother smoothed his hair and told them other stories.

In the evening, when little Kay was back at home and half undressed, he climbed onto the chair by the window and looked out through the little hole. A few snowflakes were drifting outside; then one of these, much larger than the rest, settled on the edge of the window box outside.

This snowflake grew and grew until it seemed to take the shape of a lady dressed in the finest white gauze, which was in fact made 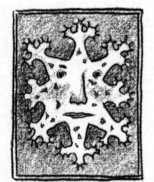 up of millions of tiny starlike flakes. She was so beautiful, wonderfully delicate and grand, but she was of ice all through, dazzling, glittering ice—and yet she was alive. Her eyes blazed out like two bright stars, but there was no peace or rest in them. Now she nodded toward the window and beckoned with her hand. The little boy was frightened and jumped down from the chair, and then he thought he saw a great bird go flying past.

The next day was clear and frosty; after that the thaw began, then it was spring. The sun shone; the first green shoots appeared; swallows built their nests; the windows were thrown open, and the two children sat once more in their little roof garden.

The roses were so beautiful that summer, more than ever before. The little girl had learned a hymn that had a line about roses, and these made her think of her own. She sang the verse to the little boy, and he sang it, too:

"In the vale the rose grows wild;
  Children play all the day —
  One of them is the Christ child."

How lovely the summer was. The rose garden seemed as if it would never stop flowering.

Kay and Gerda were sitting looking at a picture book of birds and animals, and then — just as the clock in the great church tower began to strike five — Kay said, "Oh! Something pricked me in my heart! Oh! Now I've got something in my eye!"

The little girl put her arm around his neck, and he blinked his eyes. But no, there was nothing to be seen.

"I think it's gone," he said. But it wasn't. It was one of those tiny splinters from the demon's looking glass — I'm sure you remember it. Poor Kay! He had gotten another piece right in his heart, which would soon be like a lump of ice. He didn't feel it hurting now, but it was there all right.

"Why are you crying?" he asked. "It makes you look horribly ugly. There's nothing the matter with me. Ugh!" he cried suddenly. "That rose has a worm in it. And look at that one — it's crooked. They're rotten, all of them. So are the boxes, too." And then he kicked the box hard and tore off the two roses.

"Kay, what are you doing?" cried the little girl. And when he saw how frightened she was, he tore off a third rose, and ran in at his window, away from his little friend Gerda.

After that, when she brought out the picture book, he said that it was baby stuff. When the grandmother told them stories, he would always find fault and argue. He would even walk close behind her, put on spectacles, and mimic her way of talking. It was so well done that it made the people laugh. Soon he could mimic the ways of everyone in the street, especially if they were odd or unpleasant. People used to say, "Oh, he's clever, that boy!" But all this came from the splinters of glass in his eye and in his heart; they made him tease even little Gerda, who loved him more than anything in the world.

His games had become quite different now; they were so scientific and practical. One winter's day, as the snowflakes drifted down, he brought out a magnifying glass, then held out the corner of his blue jacket to catch some falling flakes.

"Now look through the glass, Gerda," he said. And she saw that every flake was very much larger, and looked like a splendid flower or a ten-pointed star. It was certainly a wonderful sight. "Look at that pattern — isn't it marvelous!" said Kay. "These are much more interesting than real flowers — and there isn't a single fault in them. They're perfect — if only they didn't melt."

A little later Kay came back wearing big gloves and carrying his sled on his back. He shouted into Gerda's ear, "They're letting me go tobogganing in the town square where the others are playing!" And away he went.

Out in the square the boldest boys would often tie their sleds to farmers' carts, and so be pulled along for quite a ride. It was enormous fun. This time, while their games were in full swing, a very large sled arrived; it was painted white all over, and in it sat a figure muffled up in a white fur cloak and wearing a white fur hat. This sled drove twice round the square, but moving quickly, Kay managed to fix his own sled behind it, and a swift ride began. The big sled went faster and faster, then turned off into the next street. The driver looked around and nodded to Kay in the friendliest fashion, just as if they had always known each other. Every time that Kay thought of unfastening his sled, the driver would turn and nod to him again, so he kept still.

On they drove, straight out of the city gates. And now the snow began to fall so thick and fast that the little boy couldn't even see his hand in front of him as they rushed along. At last he *did* manage to untie the rope, but it was of no use: his little sled still clung to the big one, and they sped along like the wind. He cried out at the top of his voice, but no one heard him; the snow fell, and the sled raced on. From time to time it seemed to jump, as if they were going over dykes and hedges. Terror seized him; he tried to say the Lord's Prayer, but all he could remember was multiplication tables. The snowflakes grew bigger and bigger, until at last they looked like great white birds. All at once they swerved to one side; the sled came to a halt, and the driver stood up. The white fur cloak and cap were all of snow, and the driver — ah, she was a lady, tall and slender, dazzlingly white! She was the Snow Queen herself.

"We've come far and fast," she said. "But you must be frozen. Creep under my bearskin cloak." She put him beside her in the sled and wrapped the cloak around him; he felt as if he were sinking into a snowdrift. "Are you still cold?" she asked, and she kissed him on the forehead. Ahhh! Her kiss was

162

colder than ice; it went straight to his heart, which was already halfway to being a lump of ice. He felt as if he were dying, but only for a moment. Then he felt perfectly well, and he no longer noticed the cold.

"My sled! Don't forget my sled!" That was the first thought that came to him. So it was tied to one of the big white birds, which flew along with the little sled on its back. The Snow Queen kissed Kay once again, and after that he had no memory of Gerda or the grandmother, or of anyone at home.

"Now I must give you no more kisses," said the Snow Queen, "or you will be kissed to death."

Kay looked at her. She was so beautiful; he could not imagine a wiser, lovelier face. She no longer seemed to him to be made of ice, as she once had seemed when she came to the attic window and waved to him. Now, in his eyes, she was perfect, and he felt no fear. He told her that he could do mental arithmetic, and fractions, too, that he knew the square miles of all the principal countries, and the number of inhabitants. As he talked, she smiled at him, until he began to think that what he knew was, after all, not quite so much. And he looked up into the vast expanse of the sky, as they rose up high, and she flew with him over the dark clouds, while the storm wind whistled and raved, making him think of ballads of olden times.

Over forest and lake they flew, over sea and land; beneath them screamed the icy blast; the wolves howled, the snow glittered; the black crows soared across the plains, cawing as they went. But high over all shone the great, clear, silver moon, and Kay gazed up at it all through the long, long winter night. During the day he slept at the Snow Queen's feet.

PART THE THIRD
THE ENCHANTED
FLOWER GARDEN OF THE
OLD WOMAN WHO
UNDERSTOOD MAGIC

*B*ut what of little Gerda when Kay did not return? Where could he be? No one knew; no one had any idea. The only thing the boys could say was that they had seen him tie his little sled to a big one, which drove out into the street and through the city gate. But who could tell what happened after that? There was great grief in the town; little Gerda wept many tears. Then people began to say that he must be dead, that he had fallen into the river that flowed past the city walls. Oh, what a long, dark winter it was!

At last came the spring, and the first warm sunshine.

"Kay is dead and gone," said little Gerda.

"*I* don't believe it," said the sunshine.

"He is dead and gone," she said to the swallows.

"*I* don't believe it," declared each of the swallows. And at last little Gerda didn't believe it either.

"I will put on my new red shoes," she said one morning. "The ones Kay has never seen, and I'll go down and ask the river."

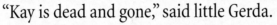

164

It was still very early when she kissed her sleeping grandmother, put on the red shoes, and walked all alone through the city gate and down to the river.

"Is it true that you have taken my little playmate?" she said. "I'll give you my red shoes if you'll let me have him back."

The waves, she thought, nodded back to her very strangely. So she took off her red shoes, the most precious things she owned, and threw them into the water. But they fell close to the bank, and the little waves carried them straight back to her. It seemed as if the river would not accept her dearest possession because it hadn't taken little Kay. But then Gerda felt that perhaps she hadn't thrown the shoes out far enough, so she climbed into a boat that lay among the rushes, went to the farther end of it, and threw the shoes again. But the boat had not been moored securely, and the movement made it float away from the shore. It began to glide away, gathering speed all the time.

At this, little Gerda was very much frightened, and she began to cry, only nobody heard her except the sparrows, and they couldn't carry her ashore. But they flew along the bank, singing as if to comfort her, "Here we are! Here we are!" On sped the boat, while little Gerda sat quite still in her stockinged feet. Her red shoes floated behind, but they couldn't catch the boat, which was now moving faster and faster.

The scene was pretty enough on both sides of the water — there were lovely flowers, old trees, and grassy meadows with sheep and cows — but there wasn't a person in sight.

Perhaps the river is carrying me to little Kay, thought Gerda, and her spirits began to rise. She stood up and gazed for hour after hour at the beautiful green banks. At last she came to a cherry orchard, in which stood a little house with curious red and blue windows and a thatched roof; standing outside were two wooden soldiers, presenting arms whenever anyone passed. Gerda called out to them, thinking that they were alive, but of course they gave no answer. The river seemed to be driving the boat toward the bank, and Gerda called out even more pleadingly. Then, from the cottage, came an old, old woman, leaning on a cane. She wore a large sun hat painted all over with many kinds of lovely flowers.

"You poor little child!" said the old woman. "How ever did you come to be on this river, so far out in the wide world?" And with that she stepped into the water, hooked the boat with her cane, pulled it ashore, and lifted little Gerda out. "Now come and tell me who you are," she said, "and how you managed to reach my house."

So Gerda told her everything, and the old woman shook her head and murmured, "Hm, hm!" And when Gerda had finished her tale and asked if the old woman had seen little Kay, the woman said that he hadn't yet passed by, but he was sure to come; Gerda was not to worry, but to have a taste of her cherries, and see her flowers, which were more wonderful than any picture book — every one of them had a story to tell. Then she took Gerda into the little house and locked the door.

The windows were very high up, and the glass in them was red and yellow and blue. The daylight shone very strangely into the room with all these colors. But on the table were the most delicious cherries, and Gerda was told that she could eat as many as she liked. While she was eating, the old woman combed her hair with a golden comb, and her hair curled fair and shining around her little face, which was just like a rose.

"I've often thought I would fancy a nice little girl around, just like you," said the old woman. "We shall get on very well together—you shall see." And she combed away at Gerda's hair, and as she combed, the little girl was forgetting her playmate Kay more and more. For the old woman could manage a bit of magic, though she was by no means a wicked witch. She used her magic only now and then for her own pleasure—and just now her pleasure was to keep little Gerda. To make sure of this, she went out into the garden and pointed her cane at each of the lovely rosebushes; at once, each bush sank into the black earth, as if it had never been. For the old woman feared that if Gerda saw the roses, she would think of her own in the roof boxes, remember little Kay, and run off to take up her journey.

This done, she took Gerda out into the flower garden. Ah, that garden— you cannot imagine what magical beauty and fragrance she found there. All the flowers that you could ever bring to mind were growing together in full bloom at one time. It was better than all the picture books. Gerda jumped with joy and played there until the sun went down behind the tall cherry trees. Then she was given a lovely bed, its red silk pillows stuffed with violets, and here she slept.

When morning came, she went out again to play among the flowers in the radiant sunshine, and in this way many days were spent. Before long she knew every separate flower, and yet, although there were so many, she felt that one was missing—only she could not think which. Then one day, as she was sitting indoors, her eyes turned to the painted flowers on the old woman's sun hat; the loveliest of all was a rose. The old woman had forgotten this when she had made the real ones disappear into the ground. See what happens when you don't keep your wits about you!

"Oh!" cried Gerda. "Why have I never seen any roses in the garden?" And she ran in and out of the flower beds, searching and searching, but not a rose was to be found. At last she sat down and cried, but her warm tears fell just where a rose bush had sunk into the earth. At once the bush sprang up, as full of fresh flowers as when it had disappeared. Gerda put her arms around it and kissed the roses, and thought about those in the roof garden of her home — and then she remembered Kay.

"Oh, what a lot of time I have lost!" said the little girl. "I set out to find Kay. Do you know where he is?" she asked the roses. "Do you think he is dead and gone?"

"No, he is not dead," said the roses. "We have been in the earth where the dead are, but Kay was not there."

"Oh, thank you," said Gerda; then she went over to the other flowers, looked into their cups, and asked, "Do you know where little Kay is?"

What did the convolvulus say?

"High above, overlooking the narrow mountain road, stands an ancient castle. Evergreen creepers grow thickly over the old red walls; leaf by leaf, they twine around a balcony where a fair young girl leans over the balustrade, gazing down at the path below. No rose on its branch is fresher and lovelier; no apple blossom that floats from the tree is more graceful and delicate. Listen — her silk dress rustles as she moves. 'When will he come?' she says."

"Is it Kay you mean?" asked little Gerda.

"I tell only my own story, my own dream," the convolvulus answered.

What did the little snowdrop say?

"Between the trees, a board hangs by two ropes; it's a swing. Two pretty little girls in snow-white dresses sit swinging; long, green silk ribbons are fluttering from their hats. Their brother, who is bigger than they are, is standing up in the swing with his arm around the rope to keep himself steady, for in one hand he holds a little bowl and in the other a clay pipe; he is blowing soap bubbles. To and fro goes the swing, while the bubbles float away in a rainbow of changing colors; the last one still clings to the pipe and sways in the wind. The swing still moves, to and fro. The little black dog, as light as the bubbles, leaps up on his hind legs; he wants to join the others on the swing. But it swoops past, out of reach, and the dog flops down, barking furiously. The children laugh; the bubbles burst. A swinging plank, a white flash of dissolving foam — that is my picture; that's my song."

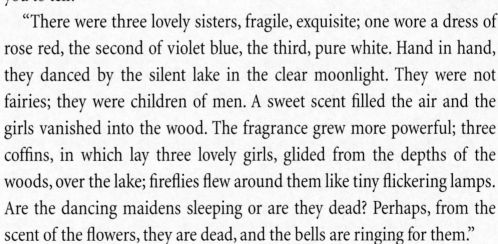

"Your story may be beautiful, but you make it sound so sad, and you don't mention little Kay at all. Hyacinths, what have you to tell?"

"There were three lovely sisters, fragile, exquisite; one wore a dress of rose red, the second of violet blue, the third, pure white. Hand in hand, they danced by the silent lake in the clear moonlight. They were not fairies; they were children of men. A sweet scent filled the air and the girls vanished into the wood. The fragrance grew more powerful; three coffins, in which lay three lovely girls, glided from the depths of the woods, over the lake; fireflies flew around them like tiny flickering lamps. Are the dancing maidens sleeping or are they dead? Perhaps, from the scent of the flowers, they are dead, and the bells are ringing for them."

"You make me feel dreadfully sad," said little Gerda. "And your own scent is so powerful that I can't help thinking of those sleeping girls. Can little Kay really be dead? The roses have been in the ground, and they say no."

"Ding dong!" rang out the hyacinth bells. "We're not ringing for little Kay; we don't know him. All we sing is our own song, the only one we know."

So Gerda went to the buttercup, which shone out from its fresh green leaves. "You are a bright little sun!" said Gerda. "Tell me if you know where I can find my playmate."

The buttercup shone very prettily and looked up at Gerda. Now, what song would the buttercup sing? Not one that gave her news of little Kay.

"In a small backyard, the heavenly sun shone bright and warm; it was the first day of spring, and the sunbeams slid down the neighbor's whitewashed wall. Nearby, the first yellow flowers of spring were growing, gleaming just like gold in the golden rays. The old grandmother sat outside in her chair; her granddaughter, a poor servant girl but pretty enough, had come home for a short visit, and now she kissed her grandmother. There was heart's gold in that kiss in the golden morning. That's all; there's my story."

"My poor old granny!" sighed Gerda. "I'm sure she's longing for me and grieving, just as she grieved for little Kay. But I'll soon be home again, and I'll bring Kay with me. It's no use asking the flowers—their own tales are all they know, and they tell me nothing at all."

She tucked up her dress so that she could run fast, and away she went. Then something struck her leg quite smartly as she leaped over it; she looked — and it was a narcissus. *Maybe* you *have news for me,* she thought, and she bent down toward the flower.

"I see myself! I see myself!" said the narcissus.

170

"Ah, what a sweet perfume! High up in her attic lodging is a little ballet dancer. She stands on tiptoe, now on one leg, now on the other, and kicks out at the world. It is all in the mind, you know. Now she pours water from the kettle onto a piece of cloth—it's her dancer's bodice; cleanliness is next to godliness, as they say. Her white dress hangs on a peg; that, too, has been washed, then hung on the roof to dry. Now she puts it on, and around her neck she ties a saffron yellow scarf. It makes the dress seem even whiter. She raises one leg high in the air. How elegantly she stands and sways on her stalk! I see myself! I see myself!"

"That is your story, not mine," said Gerda. "I don't want to hear any more." She ran to the edge of the garden. The gate was locked, but she twisted the rusty fastening until it came away; the gate flew open, and little Gerda ran out barefoot into the wide world. Three times she looked back, but nobody was following her. At last she could run no farther, so she sat down on a big stone. As she gazed around her, she realized that summer was over; it was late autumn. There had been no signs of changing time in that enchanted garden, where the bright sun always shone and flowers of every season bloomed together.

"Oh, I have lingered here too long," said little Gerda. "Autumn has come; I dare not stop!" She got up from the stone and started off once more.

How tired and sore her feet were! How cold and damp was the countryside! The long willow leaves had turned quite yellow and wet with mist; they dropped off one by one. Only the thorny sloe had kept its fruit, but that was so sour that the thought of it twisted your mouth. Oh, how mournful and bleak it was in the wide world!

PART THE FOURTH
PRINCE AND PRINCESS

Gerda soon had to rest again. And there, hopping about in the snow, right in front of her, was a raven. He had been staring at her for some time, with his head on one side, then on the other. Now he greeted her, "Caw, caw! How do, how do!" It may not have been an elegant way of speaking, but it was kindly meant. He asked her where she was going all alone in the wide world. So she told the raven the whole of her story and asked if he had seen little Kay.

The raven nodded thoughtfully and said, "Could be! Could be!"

"Oh — you really think that you have some news?" cried the little girl. And she hugged the bird so tightly that she nearly squeezed him to death.

"Caw, caw! Care-ful, care-ful!" the raven said. "I think it may have been little Kay. But I fancy that by this time he will have forgotten you for the princess."

"Does he live with a princess?" asked Gerda.

"Now listen and I'll tell you," said the raven. "But I find it so hard to talk your language. If only you understood raven speech, I could tell you better."

"No, I never learned that," said Gerda, "though my granny knew it and other strange things, too. I only wish I did."

172

"Well, never mind," said the raven. "I'll tell you as plainly as I can; you can't ask for more." And then he related what he knew.

"In the kingdom where we are now, a princess dwells. She is extremely clever; she has read all the newspapers in the world and has forgotten them again — that's how clever she is. She was sitting on her throne the other day when she happened to hear a little song. It goes like this: "Why should I not married be? Why not? Why not? Why not?" *Well, there's something to be said for that,* she thought. So she decided to find a partner, but she wanted one who could speak for himself when spoken to — one who didn't just stand and look important. That's very dull. She ordered her ladies-in-waiting to be called together (it was done by sounding a roll of drums), and when they heard her plan, they were delighted. 'What a splendid idea!' 'We were thinking something of the kind just the other day!' They went on making remarks like these. All that I'm telling you is perfectly true," said the raven. "I've a tame sweetheart who has a free run of the palace, and I heard the tale from her."

Need I tell you that the sweetheart was also a raven? Birds will be birds, and a raven's mate is a raven.

"The newspapers promptly came out with a border of hearts and the princess's monogram. They announced that any good-looking young man might come to the palace and meet the princess; the one who seemed most at home in the princess's company but who was also the best and most interesting talker — that was the one she meant to choose.

"Well, the suitors flocked to the palace — there never was such a crowd! But nobody won the prize, either the first day or the next. They could all talk smartly enough when they were out in the street, but when they came through the palace gate and saw the guards in their silver uniforms, and the footmen in gold all the way up the stairs, and the great

173

halls with their brilliant lights, they seemed to be struck dumb. And when they stood before the throne where the princess sat, they could find nothing to say but the last word she had spoken herself, and she had no wish to hear *that* again. Though once they were back in the street, it was all chatter, chatter as before.

"There was a line of suitors stretching away right from the city gate to the palace. I went over myself to have a look," went on the raven.

"But Kay, little Kay!" asked Gerda. "When did he come? Was he in that crowd?"

"Give me time! Give me time! We're coming to him! It was on the third day when a little chap appeared without horse or carriage and stepped jauntily up to the palace. His eyes were shining, just like yours; he had fine, thick, flowing hair, but his clothes, I must say, were shabby."

"That was Kay!" cried Gerda. "Oh, I have found him at last!" And she clapped her hands with joy.

"He had a little knapsack, or bundle, on his back," said the raven.

"Ah, that must have been his sled," said Gerda. "He had it when he left."

"It may have been," said the raven. "I didn't study it all that closely. But I do know from my tame sweetheart that when he reached the palace gate and saw the guards in silver and the footmen in gold, he was not in the least dismayed. He only nodded pleasantly and said to them, 'It must be dull work standing there; I'd sooner go inside.'

"The great halls blazed with light; it was enough to make anyone feel small. The young chap's boots squeaked dreadfully, but even this didn't trouble him."

"That's certainly Kay!" cried Gerda. "His boots were new, I know; I heard them squeaking in my grandmother's kitchen."

174

"Well, they squeaked, to be sure," said the raven. "But he went merrily up to the princess, who was sitting on a pearl as big as a spinning wheel; all the ladies-in-waiting, with their maids, and their maids' maids, and all the gentlemen courtiers with their serving-men and their serving-men's serving-men were ranged around her in order."

"But did Kay win the princess?" asked little Gerda.

"If I weren't a bird, I would have had a try myself, betrothed or not betrothed," the raven said. "He is said to have spoken as well as I do when I speak in my own raven language—or so my tame sweetheart tells me. He was so lively and confident; he hadn't come to woo the princess, he declared, only to hear her wise conversation. He liked it very well, and she liked him."

"Oh, that was certainly Kay," said Gerda. "He was so clever, he could do mental arithmetic with fractions! Oh, do please take me to the palace."

"That's easily said," replied the raven, "but how is it to be done? I must talk to my tame sweetheart about it; she'll be able to advise us, I have no doubt, for—let me tell you—a girl like you would never be allowed to enter in the regular way."

"Oh, I shall get in," said Gerda. "When Kay knows I am here, he'll come straight out and fetch me."

"Well," said the raven, waggling his head, "wait for me there by the stile." And off he flew.

It was late in the evening when he returned. "Ra-a-ax! Ra-a-ax!" he cawed. "I'm to give you my sweetheart's greetings, and here's a piece of bread from the kitchen; there's plenty there, and you must be hungry. It's impossible for you to get into the palace as you are, without even shoes on your feet, but don't cry. My sweetheart knows a little back staircase that leads to the royal bedroom, and she knows where to find the key!"

So they went into the garden, and along the avenue where the leaves were falling, leaf after leaf; then, when all the lights in the palace had gone out, one by one, the raven led little Gerda to a small back door.

Oh, how Gerda's heart beat with hope and fear! It was just as if she were about to do something wrong—yet all she wanted was to find out if the boy really *was* little Kay. Oh, yes, he must be Kay; she could see him in her mind so vividly with his bright, clever eyes and smooth, flowing hair; she remembered the way he used to smile when they sat together at home among the roses. Oh, he would surely be glad to see her, to hear what a long way she had come for his sake, and to know how grieved they had all been at home when he never returned. She trembled with fear and hope.

They had now reached the staircase where the tame raven was waiting; a little lamp was glimmering on a stand. Gerda curtsied, as her grandmother had taught her.

"My fiancé has spoken most charmingly of you, my dear young lady," said the tame raven, "and your life history, as we may call it, really touches the heart. If you will kindly take the lamp, I will lead the way. Straight on is best and shortest—we are not likely to meet anyone."

"Yet I can't help feeling that someone is following behind," said Gerda. And indeed, something did seem to rush along past her; it looked like a flight of shadows on the wall, horses with thin legs and flowing manes, huntsmen, lords and ladies on horseback.

"Those are only dreams," said the tame raven. "They come and take the gentry's thoughts on midnight rides, and that's a good thing, for you will be able to observe them more safely while they are asleep. But I hope that you will show a thankful heart if you do rise to fame and fortune."

"Now, now, there's no need to talk about that," said the woodland raven. They entered the first room, where the walls were hung with rose-

176

colored satin embroidered with flowers. Here, the dreams were racing past so swiftly that Gerda could not distinguish any one of the lords and ladies. Each hall that she passed through was more magnificent than the one before; then, at last, they arrived at the royal bedroom.

The ceiling was like the crown of a palm tree, with leaves of rarest crystal, and hanging from a thick gold stem in the center of the floor were two beds, each in the shape of a lily. One was white, and in this lay the princess. The other was scarlet—and in this Gerda knew that she must look for little Kay. She turned one of the red leaves over and saw a boy's brown hair. It was Kay! She cried his name aloud, holding the lamp near his face; the dreams on their wild steeds came whirling back to the sleeper; he woke—he turned his head—it was not little Kay.

No, it was not little Kay, though the prince, too, was a handsome boy. And now the princess looked out from the white lily bed and asked what was happening. Little Gerda wept as she told her story, but she did not forget to speak of the ravens and their kind help.

"You poor child," said the prince and princess, and they praised the ravens, adding, though, that they must not do it again. This time, all things considered, they would be given a reward.

"Would you like to fly away free?" the princess asked. "Or would you like a permanent place as Court Ravens, with all the odds and ends you want from the kitchens?"

Both the ravens bowed and prudently chose the permanent place, for they had to think of their old age. "It's a good thing to have something for a rainy day," they said. The prince stepped out of his bed so that Gerda could sleep in it — and who could do more than that? As Gerda slept, the dreams came flying back — but this time they looked like angels; they seemed to be drawing a sled, on which Kay was sitting, nodding at her. But this was only a dream, and it vanished as soon as she woke.

The next day she was dressed from top to toe in silk and velvet. She was invited to stay at the palace and pass delightful days, but she begged to have just a little carriage with a horse to draw it, and a pair of boots small enough for her feet; with these she could drive out into the wide world and seek little Kay.

She was given not only boots but a muff, and when she was ready to leave, in beautiful, fine, warm clothes, a new carriage of pure gold drew up before the door; on it the coat of arms of the royal pair glistened like a

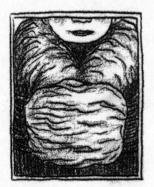

star. Coachman, footmen, and outriders — for there were outriders too — all wore gold crowns. The prince and princess personally helped her into the carriage and wished her good luck. The forest raven, who had now married his sweetheart, came along for the first twelve miles or so; he sat beside her, for he could not bear traveling backward. The tame bird stood in the gateway flapping her wings; she didn't go with them because too much rich palace fare had given her a headache. The inside of the coach was lined with iced cake and sugar candy, while the space beneath the seat was packed with fruit and ginger nuts.

"Farewell! Farewell!" cried the prince and princess, and little Gerda wept. So did the raven, and in this way they passed the first few miles. Then the raven said his own goodbye, and that was the hardest parting of them all. He flew up into a tree and flapped his black wings as long as he could see the carriage, which gleamed as bright as the sun.

PART THE FIFTH
THE LITTLE ROBBER GIRL

*T*hey drove through the dark forest, but the carriage shone like a fiery torch; it dazzled the eyes of the robber band — they could not bear it.

"It's gold! It's gold!" they roared. Then, rushing forward, they seized the horses, killed the outriders, coachman, and footmen, and dragged little Gerda out of the carriage.

"She's plump; she's a dainty dish; she's been fed on nut kernels!" said the old robber woman, who had a long, bristly beard and shaggy eyebrows hanging over her eyes. "She's as tender and sweet as a little, fat lamb. Yum, yum! She'll make a tasty dinner!" She drew out a bright, sharp knife, which glittered quite dreadfully.

"Ouch!" screeched the hag all at once. She had been bitten in the ear by her own little daughter, who hung on her back and who was so wild and mischievous that she was quite out of hand. "You loathsome brat!" said her mother, and she forgot what she had meant to do with Gerda.

"She shall be my playmate," said the little robber girl. "She shall give

179

me her muff and her pretty clothes and sleep with me in my bed." And so spoiled and willful was she that of course she had her own way. She got in the coach with Gerda, and away they drove, through bush and briar, deeper and deeper into the forest. The little girl was no taller than Gerda,

but much sturdier, with broader shoulders and darker skin. Her eyes were quite black, with a curious look of melancholy in them. She put her arm around little Gerda and said, "They shan't kill you — not as long as I don't get cross with you. You're a princess, I suppose?"

"No," said little Gerda, and again she told all her adventures, and how fond she was of little Kay. The robber girl watched her seriously and nodded. "They shan't kill you even if I do get cross with you," she said. "I'll do it myself." Then she dried Gerda's eyes and put both her hands into the pretty muff, which was so soft and warm.

Suddenly the carriage stopped; they had reached the courtyard of a robber's castle. Its walls were cracked from top to bottom, and crows and ravens were flying out of the gaps and holes, while huge hounds, each one looking as if he could swallow a man, leaped high into the air, but not a single bark came from them, for that was forbidden. In the great old hall, cobwebbed and black with soot, a large fire burned on the stone floor; the smoke drifted about under the roof, trying to find its own way out. A vast cauldron of soup was bubbling away; hares and rabbits were roasting on turning spits.

"Tonight you shall sleep with me and all my pets," said the robber girl. First they had something to eat and drink, then they went over to a corner where straw and blankets were scattered. Above them, in holes and on ledges, about a hundred pigeons were roosting; they seemed to be asleep, but a slight stir ran through them when the little girls appeared.

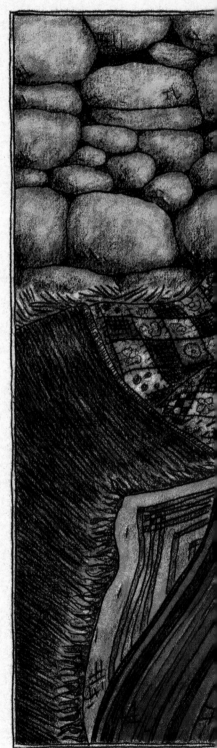

"They're mine — all of them," said the little robber girl. She seized one of the nearest, took it by the legs, and shook it until it flapped its wings. "Kiss it!" she cried, waving it in Gerda's face. Then she pointed to some wooden bars nailed over a hole above their heads. "Those are woodland riffraff, both of them. They'd fly off in a flash if they weren't locked up. And here's my special sweetheart, Bae." She pulled a reindeer forward by the horn; it was tethered to the wall, with a shiny copper ring around its neck. "He's another one who'd fly off if we didn't keep him prisoner. Every night I tickle his neck with my sharp knife — he doesn't care for that!" And, drawing a long knife out of a crack in the wall, she ran it lightly across the reindeer's neck. The poor creature struggled and kicked, but the robber girl laughed and pulled Gerda down with her under the rug.

"Are you taking that knife into bed with you?" Gerda asked as she looked at it nervously.

"I always sleep with a knife at hand," said the little robber girl. "You never know what may happen. But now tell me again about little Kay and why you came out into the wide world."

So Gerda told her tale once more, from the very beginning, and the woodland pigeons moaned in their cage, and the other pigeons slept. Then the little robber girl fell asleep, too, one arm around

181

Gerda's neck, the other holding the knife; you could hear from her breathing that she slept. But Gerda couldn't even close her eyes, not knowing whether she was to live or die. The robbers sat around the fire and drank and sang, and the robber woman turned somersaults. It was a frightful sight to behold.

Then all at once the woodland pigeons cried, "Rr-coo! Mm-coo! We have seen little Kay! A white hen was carrying his sled, and he was sitting in the Snow Queen's carriage, which swept low over the forest where we lay in the nest. She breathed down on us young ones, and all except the two of us here froze to death. Rr-coo! Mm-coo!"

"What are you saying up there?" cried Gerda. "Which way did the Snow Queen go? Can you tell me?"

"She must have been making for Lapland, for you'll always find snow and ice there. You ask the reindeer; he's sure to know."

"Yes, it's a land of ice and snow — everything there is lovely and pleasant," the reindeer said. "You can run and leap to your heart's delight in the great shining valleys. There the Snow Queen has her summer palace, but her real home is in a castle far, far off toward the North Pole, on an island called Spitzbergen."

"Oh, Kay, poor Kay!" sighed Gerda.

"Lie still, you," said the robber girl, "or you'll get my knife in your middle!"

When morning came, Gerda told her all that the pigeons had said. The little robber girl looked very grave, but she nodded and said, "Never mind, never mind; it doesn't matter. . . . Do you know where Lapland is?" she asked the reindeer.

"Who should know better than I?" said the reindeer, and his eyes shone at the thought of it. "I was born and bred in that land; once I could leap and play freely there in the snowfields."

"Listen to me," said the robber girl to Gerda. "All our menfolk are out. My old ma's still here, and here she'll stay — but later in the morning she'll take a swig from that big bottle, and after that she'll have forty winks. Then I'll see what I can do for you." She jumped out of bed, ran across to her mother, pulled her by the beard, and called, "Good morning, my dear old nanny goat!" Her mother flipped her on the nose, making it quite red and blue — but it was all for sheer affection.

Then, when her mother had had a drink from the bottle and was taking a nap, the robber girl went over to the reindeer. "I'd love to go on teasing you a few more times with that sharp knife of mine, because you always look so funny when I do, but never mind — I'm going to set you free so that you can run to Lapland. But you must take this little girl to the Snow Queen's palace, where her playmate is. I expect you've heard her story; she was talking loudly enough, and you are always one for eavesdropping."

The reindeer leaped for joy. The robber girl lifted Gerda onto his back, taking care to tie her firmly on, with a little cushion for a seat.

"You'll be all right," she said. "Here are your fur boots — you'll need them in that cold — but I shall keep your muff; it's far too pretty to lose. Still, you won't have to freeze — here are my mother's big gloves. They'll reach right up to your elbows. Shove your hands in! Now they look just like my ugly old mother's!"

Gerda wept with happiness.

"I can't stand that sniveling," said the robber girl. "You ought to be looking really pleased. Here are two loaves and a ham, so you won't starve." These provisions were tied to the reindeer's back. Then the robber girl opened the door and called in the big dogs. After that she cut the rope with her knife and said to the reindeer, "Off you go! But take good care of the little girl!"

Gerda stretched out her hands in the enormous gloves and called "Goodbye!" to the robber girl, and the reindeer sped away past bush and briar, through the great forest, over marsh and moor, and the wide plains, as swiftly as he could go. The wolves howled; the ravens screamed; the sky seemed filled with sneezing, crackling noises — *Schooo, schooo! Piff, piff!* — each time with a glow of red. "Those are my dear old northern lights," said the reindeer. "Aren't they beautiful!" Faster and faster he ran, through the night, through the day. The loaves were finished, and so was the ham — and then they were in Lapland.

PART THE SIXTH

THE LAPLAND WOMAN
AND THE
FINMARK WOMAN

They stopped at a little hut, a wretched place; the roof nearly touched the ground, and the door was so low that the family had to get down on all fours to crawl in and out. Nobody was at home except an old Lapp woman, who was frying fish over an oil lamp. The reindeer told her Gerda's story, but first it told its own, which seemed the more important. Gerda was too frozen with cold to speak at all.

"Oh, you poor things!" cried the Lapland woman. "You've a long way to go yet. You still have several hundred miles to cross before you get to Finmark — that's where the Snow Queen is just now, sending off those fireworks of hers every night. I'll write you a few words on a piece of dried codfish — I've got no paper — and you take it to the Finnwoman

184

living up there. She can tell you better than I can what to do." And so, when Gerda was properly warm and had had some supper, the Lapland woman wrote some words on a piece of dried cod and told Gerda to take good care of it. Then she fastened her on the reindeer's back again, and off they sped. *Schooo, schooo! Crack, crack!* came the noises from the sky, and all night long the glorious northern lights flashed violet blue. At last they arrived in Finmark and knocked on the Finnwoman's chimney, for she hadn't even a door.

Inside, it was so swelteringly hot that the Finnwoman wore hardly a stitch of clothing. She was small and dumpy, with a brownish skin. The first thing she did was to loosen little Gerda's clothes, and take off her boots and thick gloves; then she laid a piece of ice on the reindeer's head. Then she studied what was written on the dried-fish letter. She read it three times; after that she knew it by heart, and she dropped it into the cooking pot, for she never wasted anything.

The reindeer now told his story, and after that, little Gerda's, and the Finnwoman's wise eyes twinkled, but she didn't say a word.

"Ah, you're so clever," said the reindeer. "I know you can tie up all the winds in the world with a single thread. When the captain undoes the first knot, he gets a fair wind; if he undoes the second, then gusts begin to blow; if he undoes the third and fourth, a gale roars up that hurls down the forest trees and wrecks the ship. Won't you make this little girl a magic drink that will give her the strength of twelve men, so that she can overcome the Snow Queen?"

"The strength of twelve men?" said the Finmark woman. "A lot of good *that* would do!" She went over to a shelf and took down a rolled-up parchment. She opened it out; strange letters were written on it, and she read so intently that sweat ran from her brow like rain.

But the reindeer went on pleading so hard for little Gerda, and Gerda looked at her with such tearful, beseeching eyes, that once again she turned her gaze on them. Then, drawing the reindeer into a corner, she put fresh ice on his head and whispered in his ear, "Little Kay is with the Snow Queen, sure enough; he finds everything there to his liking, and thinks that he's in the finest place in the world—but all that is because he has a splinter of glass in his heart, and another in his eye. These must come out or he'll stay bewitched, and the Snow Queen will keep her hold over him forever!"

"But is there nothing that you can give little Gerda to break that hold?"

"I cannot give her greater power than she has already. Don't you see how great that is? How men and beasts all feel that they must serve her? How far she has come in the wide world on her own bare feet? She must not learn of her power; it comes from her own heart, from her being a

dear and innocent child. If she can't find her own way into the Snow Queen's palace and free little Kay, there is nothing that we can do to help. Now! About ten miles farther north is the edge of the Snow Queen's garden. You can carry the little girl as far as that, then put her down by the big bush with red berries, standing in the snow; don't stay gossiping, but hurry back here." With that, the Finnwoman lifted little Gerda onto the reindeer's back, and off he dashed as fast as his legs could go.

"Oh! I've left my boots behind! And my gloves!" cried little Gerda. She felt stung by the piercing cold. But the reindeer dared not stop; on he ran till he came to the big bush with the red berries. There he put Gerda down, and he kissed her on the lips; as he did so, great shining tears ran down the poor animal's face. Then he turned and sped back as fast as he was able.

And there was poor Gerda, without boots, without gloves, in the midst of that terrible icy land and its piercing cold. She started to run forward, but a whole regiment of snowflakes appeared in front of her. They had not fallen from above, for the sky was quite clear, sparkling with northern lights. These flakes came running along the ground, and the nearer they came, the larger they grew. Gerda remembered how strange and wonderfully made the flakes had seemed when she'd looked at them through the magnifying glass. How long ago that was. But these were far bigger and much more frightening— they were the Snow Queen's frontier guards. They had the weirdest, most fantastic shapes. Some were like huge wild hedgehogs; others were like knotted bunches of snakes writhing their heads in all directions; others again were like fat little bears with icicles for hair. All of them were glistening white; all were living snowflakes.

Then little Gerda began to say the Lord's Prayer, and the cold was so intense that she could see her own breath—it rose from her mouth like a cloud. The cloud became thicker and thicker, and took the form of little bright angels who grew the moment they touched the ground. On their heads were helmets; in their hands were spears and shields. By the time Gerda had finished her prayer, she was encircled by a whole legion of these spirits. They struck out at the dreadful snow-things, shattering them into hundreds of pieces, and Gerda was able to go on her way without fear or danger. The angels patted her feet and hands so that she hardly felt the biting cold, and she hurried on toward the Snow Queen's palace.

187

But now we must see how little Kay was faring. Whatever his thoughts, they were not of Gerda; he certainly did not dream that she was just outside the palace.

The palace walls were of driven snow, and the doors and windows of cutting wind. There were over a hundred halls, just as the drifting snow had formed them; the largest stretched for miles. All were lit by the brilliant northern lights; they were vast, empty, glittering, bleak as ice, and deathly

cold. In the very midst of the palace there was a frozen lake; it had split into a thousand pieces, but each piece was so exactly like the next that it seemed not an accident but a cunning work of art. The Snow Queen always sat in the center of this lake whenever she was at home; she used to say that she was on the Mirror of Reason: the best glass—indeed, the only that mattered—in the world.

Little Kay was quite blue with cold; in fact, he was nearly black. But he never noticed, for the Snow Queen had kissed away his shivering, and his heart was hardly more than a lump of ice. He was busily dragging about some sharp, flat pieces of ice, arranging them in every possible pattern. What he was trying to do was to make a special word, and this he could never manage, try as he would. The word was ETERNITY.

For the Snow Queen had said to him, "If you can spell out *that* for me, you shall be your own master, and I will make you a present of the whole world, together with a new pair of skates." But he still could not manage it.

"Now I must fly off to the warm lands," said the Snow Queen. "I want to take a peep into the black cauldrons." (She meant the volcanoes Etna and Vesuvius.) "I shall whiten their tops a little — it does them good after all those lemons and grapes." Off she flew, and Kay was left quite alone in the vast empty hall, gazing at the pieces of ice, and thinking, thinking, until his head seemed to crack. There he sat, stiff and still; anyone might have thought he was frozen to death.

It was just then that little Gerda stepped into the palace through the great doors of cutting winds. But she said her evening prayer, and the cold winds dropped as if they were falling asleep. She entered the vast, cold, empty hall — and there was Kay! She knew him at once; she rushed toward him and flung her arms about his neck and held him tight, crying, "Kay! Dear little Kay! I've found you at last!"

But he sat there quite still, stiff, and cold.

Then Gerda began to weep hot tears, which fell on his breast and reached right through to his heart. There, they thawed the lump of ice, and washed away the splinter of glass. Kay looked up at her, and she sang the verse that they used to sing together:

> "*In the vale the rose grows wild;*
> *Children play all the day —*
> *One of them is the Christ child.*"

Then tears came into Kay's eyes, too. And, as he cried, the splinter of

glass was washed away; now he could recognize her, and he cried out joyfully, "Gerda! Dear little Gerda! Where have you been all this time? And what has been happening to me?" He looked around him. "How cold it is! How huge and empty!" The air was so filled with their happiness that even the pieces of ice began dancing for sheer delight, and when they were tired and lay down again, they formed the very word that the Snow Queen had told Kay to make — the one for which he would be his own master, and be given the whole world and a new pair of skates.

Then Gerda kissed his cheeks, and their color came back to them; she kissed his eyes, and they shone like hers; she kissed his hands and feet, and he was well and sound and warm, the Kay she had always known. The Snow Queen could now come back as soon as she liked — Kay's sign of release was there, laid out in shining letters of ice.

Hand in hand, they walked out of the great echoing palace. Wherever they went, the winds were still and the sun broke out. When they reached the bush with the red berries, there stood the reindeer, waiting for them. With him was a young doe, and she gave warm milk to the boy and girl. Then the reindeer and the doe carried Kay and Gerda first to the Finmark woman, where they warmed themselves in the hot room and were given advice about the journey home, and then to the Lapland woman. She had made new clothes for them and had prepared a sled.

The reindeer and the doe bounded along right up to the borders of their country. There, Kay and Gerda could see the first green shoots of spring coming out of the ground; the sled could go no farther, and the reindeer and the Lapland woman had to return to the north. "Farewell! Farewell! Goodbye! Goodbye!" said each and all.

The first little birds of spring began to twitter, the first green leaves appeared on the forest trees, and through the wood came a young girl riding a splendid horse. Gerda knew that horse, for it had been harnessed

to her golden coach. The young girl had a scarlet cap on her head and pistols at her side. She was the robber girl! She was tired of home life, she told them, and was making for the North; if she did not like it there, she would try some other direction. She recognized Gerda at once, and Gerda recognized her; they were both delighted to meet each other again.

"You're a fine one to go straying off like that!" she said to

Kay. "I wonder if you deserve to have anyone running to the ends of the earth for your sake!"

But Gerda patted her cheek and asked after the prince and princess.

"They've gone traveling to foreign parts," said the robber girl.

"And the raven?"

"Oh, the raven's dead," she replied. "His tame sweetheart's a widow now and wears a piece of black wool on her leg. She's always moaning and groaning, but it doesn't mean a thing. Now you tell me your adventures, and how you managed to find him." And Gerda and Kay both told their separate tales.

"Well, well, well: today's mishap is tomorrow's story," said the robber girl. She took each of them by the hand and promised that if she ever passed through their hometown, she would pay them a visit. Then she rode off and away, into the wide world.

But Kay and Gerda went on, hand in hand. As they went, the spring flowered around them, beautiful with blossoms and green leaves. They heard the church bells ringing; they saw ahead the towers and walls of a city; they were nearing home.

And they entered the town; they went up the stairs of the grandmother's house and into the room near the roof, where everything stood just where it was before, and the clock still said, "Tick tock," and the hands still marked the hours. But as they went through the door, they noticed that they themselves had grown; they were not young children. The roses in the wooden boxes were flowering in at the open window, and out there were their own little wooden stools. Kay and Gerda sat down on them and held each other's hands. The terrible icy splendor of the Snow Queen's palace had slipped away from their minds like a distant dream. Grandmother sat beside them in the heavenly sunshine and read to them from the Bible, "Except ye become as little children, ye shall not enter into the Kingdom of Heaven."

Kay and Gerda looked into each other's eyes, and at once they remembered the old song, and saw its meaning:

> *"In the vale the rose grows wild;*
> *Children play all the day—*
> *One of them is the Christ child."*

So there they sat together, the same children still at heart. And it was summer, warm delightful summer....

A wood engraving of "a poor little girl" selling matches on a wintry street prompted the writing of this tale. The publisher, who wanted a Christmas story for his almanac, had given Andersen the choice of three pictures: this was promptly chosen. The tale was later included in Andersen's 1848 booklet. (It also contained "The Old House," Dickens's favorite Andersen story.) Like Dickens, Andersen was always moved by poverty. He had known cold and hunger himself as a teenager, while roaming Copenhagen trying to place his numerous manuscripts or find work at the theater. And his mother had also told him how, as a child, she was sent out to beg in the cold and dared not return if she had earned no money.

The grandmother was based on his own dear, gentle, blue-eyed grandmother, the most sensitive and intelligent of his few relatives — excepting her son, Andersen's father. She was now dead, but lives again in this story.

Andersen also knew by now the rich tables that he describes so well. He wrote the tale while staying at Graasten Castle, one of the many aristocratic homes that welcomed this entertaining guest while on his way to "foreign lands." He felt some twinges of shame at the wealth around him while he wrote this story — but it may have stirred his imagination.

A critic who had heard both Dickens's reading of Little Nell's death and Andersen's reading of "The Little Match Girl" declared that he wept at both, but found Andersen's the more moving. With Dickens, you were always conscious of the man — not so with Andersen. Sadly we have no recordings of either man's voice, though photographs are plentiful.

*I*T WAS DREADFULLY COLD. SNOW WAS FALLING; soon it would be quite dark. It was also the very last evening of the year — New Year's Eve. In this cold and darkness, a poor little girl was wandering along, with bare head and bare feet. It's true that she had slippers on when she left home — but what good was that? They were great big things, those slippers; they had belonged to her mother, so it is not surprising that they had fallen off when she scurried across the road, just missing two carts that were thundering past. One slipper was nowhere to be found, and a boy ran off with the other. It would do for a cradle when he had children of his own, he called out teasingly.

So there was the little girl treading along on naked feet that were quite blue with cold. In an old apron she carried a pile of matches, and she held one bunch of them in her hand. She had sold nothing the whole of the day; no one had given her a single penny. Hungry and frozen, she trudged along looking miserable. Poor little thing! The snowflakes fell on her long, fair hair, which curled so prettily at her neck. But she certainly wasn't thinking about her looks. Lights were shining in every window and wonderful smells of roasting goose drifted down the street. For it was New Year's Eve, remember, and that's what she was thinking about.

In a sheltered corner between two houses, one jutting out a little farther than the other, she crouched down and huddled herself together, tucking up her legs — but this didn't help; she grew colder and colder. She didn't dare go home, for she had sold no matches. She hadn't a single copper coin to bring back, so her father would beat her. Besides, her home was freezing, too. It was an attic under the roof, and the wind whistled through that, though the worst cracks had been stuffed with straw and rags.

Her hands were quite numb with cold. A match flame would be such a

comfort. Oh, if only she dared to strike one match, just one. She took one and struck it against the wall — *crrritch!* How it crackled and blazed! What a lovely warm clear flame, just like a little candle! She held her hand around it. Really, it was a wonderful light. The little girl seemed to be sitting in front of a big iron stove with shining brass knobs and fittings;

inside was such a warm friendly fire. Oh, what had happened? She had just put out her toes to warm them, too, when — the flame went out. The stove had gone! She was sitting in the cold with the stump of a burned-out matchstick in her hand.

She struck another match. It flared up brightly; where it shone, the wall became transparent as gauze. She could see

right into the room, where the table was laid with a shining starched white cloth; on it were dishes of finest porcelain. A delicious hot fragrance rose from a roast goose stuffed with prunes and apples. The goose seemed nearer and nearer — she could almost touch it. Then the match went out. All she could see and feel was the cold, unfriendly wall.

197

She struck another. Now she was sitting under the loveliest of Christmas trees, even bigger and more beautifully decorated than the great tree she had seen at Christmas through the glass door of the rich merchant's shop. Thousands of candles were alight on its branches, and brightly colored Christmas pictures, just like the ones in all the shop windows, were looking down at her kindly. The little girl reached out her hands—then the match burned out. But the flames from the candles seemed to rise higher and higher, and she saw that they were the stars in the heavens, high above. One of them rushed across, leaving a fiery streak in the dark night sky.

"Someone is dying!" said the little girl. Her grandmother, now dead, the only person who had ever been kind to her, had told her once that whenever a star falls, it is a sign that a soul is going to God.

She struck another match on the wall. As it lit up the blackness all around, she saw in its bright glow her dear grandmother. How sweet she looked, so loving and so kind.

"Oh, Granny, take me with you," she cried. "I know you'll disappear when the match goes out, just like the warm stove and the roast goose and the wonderful Christmas tree!" And without stopping, she struck all the rest of the matches in the bundle. Her grandmother must not go!

The flames shone out so brilliantly that all around was even brighter than daylight. Never before had her grandmother looked so tall and beautiful. She took the little girl in her arms and flew with her in joy and splendor up and up to where there is no cold, no fear, no hunger — up to heaven.

In the cold early morning, huddled in a corner, there sat the little girl, with red cheeks and smiling lips — frozen to death on the last night of the old year. The new year dawned on the little dead body with its lapful of matches; one bundle was burned out. "She was trying to warm herself," people said. No one knew what lovely things she had seen, and how gloriously she had flown with her grandmother into her own new year. ⌒╳

199

The Goblin at the Grocer's

*S*urprisingly, this sparkling little tale, at once lighthearted and profound, has a later date than almost all of the favorites—which is perhaps why it is less well known. (It was published in 1853, the sixty-fifth of the stories.) Yet the idea could have been in Andersen's mind much earlier. The setting goes back to an event in his life that he was not likely to ever forget. At seventeen, a scarecrow-like figure over six feet tall, he was obliged to make up his missed basic education at a grim provincial school, where he was kept as a kind of boarding prisoner in the unkempt house of the sadistic headmaster. Andersen dared not complain to his severe guardian, Jonas Collin, but at last a young teacher did the task for him, and braved Collin personally. At once Andersen (now twenty) was told to pack and leave. He was then allowed enough money to rent a small attic room in Copenhagen, where, with a tutor, he would complete his studies. This was a paradise for Andersen, and it lives again in the tale.

And the goblin? He was a kind of brownie, or pixie, a Danish house spirit, who (in this tale) lives happily enough with the grocer, who, every year, gives him a bowl of porridge containing a lump of butter. But one day he notices the student who rents the attic room, giving up his meager supper in exchange for a book of poems, which the grocer has been using as wrapping paper! Up the stairs he goes, and peers through the keyhole of the attic door. Amazing! From the book rises a radiant light; sweet music fills the room. Surely I must make my home here, thinks the goblin. But then he remembers the porridge. This teasing tale is about many things, but one is certainly the problem of making a choice: something, small or large, that at some time affects us all. Andersen, is, of course, both the goblin and the student.

T HERE WAS ONCE A STUDENT, a proper student; he lived in an attic and owned nothing at all. There was also a grocer, a proper grocer; he lived on the ground floor and owned the whole house. And so it was with the grocer that the goblin chose to make his home. Besides, every Christmas he was given a bowl of porridge with a great lump of butter in it. The grocer could manage that easily, and so the goblin stayed in the shop. There's a moral there somewhere, if you look for it.

One evening the student came in through the back door to buy some candles and cheese. His shopping was quickly done and paid for, and the grocer and his wife nodded, "Good evening." The wife could do more than nod, though: she was a chatterbox — talk, talk, talk. She had what they call the gift of gab; there's no doubt about that. The student nodded back — and then his eye fell on something written on the paper wrapped around the cheese, and he stood there reading it. It was a page torn from an old book, one that should never have been torn up at all, an old book full of poetry.

"There's more of that book if you want it," said the grocer. "I gave an old woman some coffee beans for it. You can have the rest for sixpence if you like."

"Thank you," said the student. "Let me have it instead of the cheese. I can do very well with bread. It's a shame to use such a book for wrapping paper! You are an excellent man, a practical man—but you have no more idea of poetry than that tub over there."

Now, this was a rude thing to say, especially the part about the tub, but the grocer laughed and the student laughed; after all, it was only a kind of joke. But the little goblin was annoyed that anyone should dare speak like that to the grocer—his landlord, too—an important person who owned the whole house and sold the best-quality butter.

That night, when the shop was shut and everyone but the student had gone to bed, the goblin tiptoed in and borrowed the gift of gab from the grocer's wife, for she had no need of it while she was asleep. Then, whatever object he put it on in the room would be able to voice its views

and opinions quite as well as the lady herself. But only one thing at a time could have it, and that was a blessing; otherwise they would have all been chattering away at once.

First, the goblin placed the gift of gab on the tub where the old newspapers were kept. "Is it really true," he asked, "that you don't know what poetry is?"

"Of course I know!" said the tub. "It's something you find at the bottom of the page in a newspaper; people cut it out. I rather think that I have more poetry in me than the student has—yet I'm only a humble tub compared with the grocer."

Then the goblin placed the gift of gab on the coffee mill. Goodness, how it clattered on! After that, he put it on the butter cask, then the cash till. They all echoed the views of the tub, and the view of the majority has to be respected.

"Now I can put that student in his place," said the goblin, and he tiptoed softly up the back staircase to the attic where the student lived. There was a light inside, and the goblin peeped through the keyhole and saw the young man reading the tattered book from the shop.

But how bright it was in the room! Out of the book rose a shining beam of light; it became a tree stem, the trunk of a noble tree that soared up and spread its branches over the student. The leaves were fresh and green, and every flower was the face of a lovely girl. Some had dark, mysterious eyes; some had eyes of sparkling blue. Every fruit was a shining star, and the air was filled with an indescribably beautiful sound of singing.

The little goblin had never seen or known of such wonders; he could never have imagined them, even. And so he stayed at the door, standing on tiptoe, peeping in, gazing and gazing, until the light in the room went out. The student must have blown out his candle and gone to bed — but still the goblin could not tear himself away; his head rang with the marvelous music, which still echoed in the air, lulling the student to sleep.

"This is beyond belief," said the goblin to himself. "I certainly never expected anything of the kind. I think I shall stay in the attic with the student." And then he pondered awhile, and then he sighed. "One must be sensible," he said. "The student hasn't any porridge."

And so — yes — he went down again to the grocer's shop. It was a good thing he did, because the tub had nearly worn out the gift of gab, what with telling everyone all the news and views of the papers stacked inside. It had done so from one angle, and was just about to turn over and gabble it all again from another, when the goblin took the gab back to the sleeping wife.

204

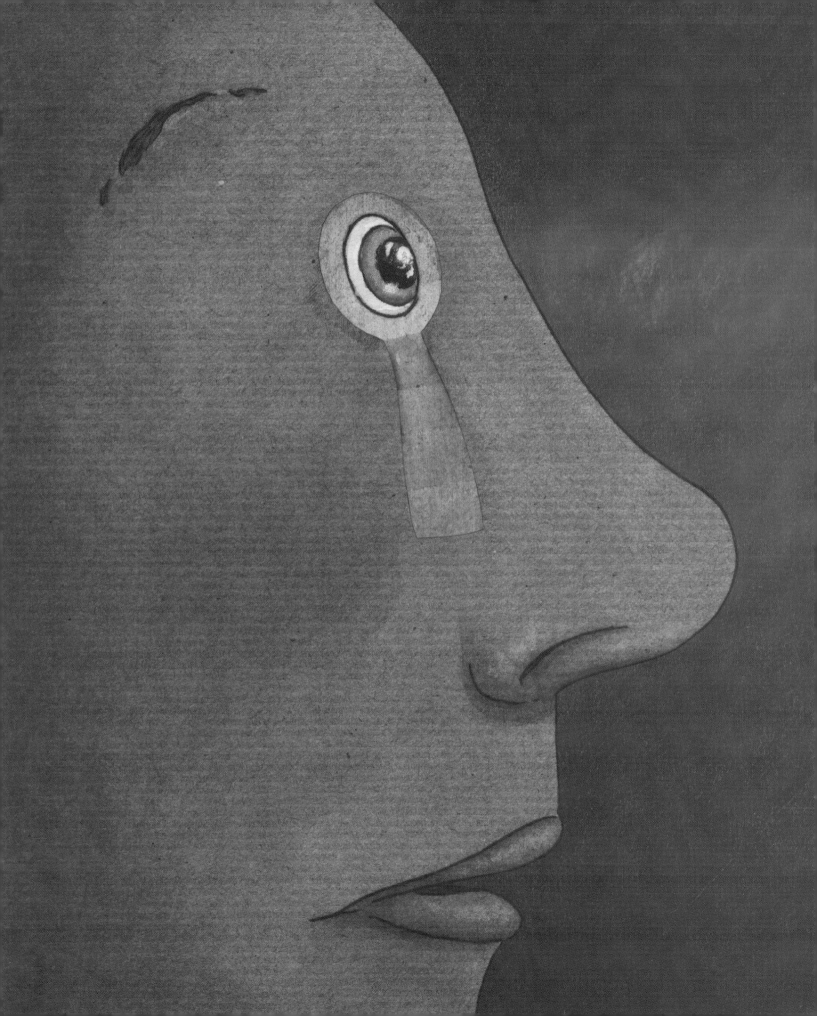

And from that time on, the whole shop, from the cash till to the firewood, took all their opinions from the tub; they held it in such respect that, ever after, when the grocer was reading out criticisms of plays or books from the newspapers, they thought that he had learned it all from the tub.

But the goblin could no longer sit quietly listening to all the wisdom and good sense that was uttered down in the shop. No — the moment the light began to shine through the attic door, he seemed to be drawn there by powerful strings, and up he had to go and station himself at the keyhole. And each time that he did this, a sense of unutterable grandeur would sweep through him — the kind of feeling that we might have at the sight of a stormy sea whose waves are so wild that God himself might be riding over them in the blast. How wonderful it would be to sit under the tree with the student! But that could never be.

Meanwhile, he was grateful to have the keyhole. He gazed through it every night, standing there on the bleak landing even when the autumn winds blew through the skylight, making him nearly freeze with cold. Yet he felt nothing of this until the light went out in the attic room and the music faded away in the howling of the wind. *Brrr!* Then he would realize how cold he was, and would creep down again to his secret corner of the shop, where it was so snug and warm. Soon there would be the Christmas bowl of porridge with its great lump of butter. Yes — the grocer was the one to choose after all.

But late one night, the goblin was woken up by a frightful commotion. People were banging at the shutters; the watchman was blowing his whistle; a fire had broken out, and the whole street seemed ablaze. Which house was burning? This one or the next? Where *was* the fire? What screams! What panic! What a fuss! The grocer's wife was so flustered that she took her gold earrings from her ears and put them in her pocket, so

that she might at least save *some*thing. The grocer dashed after his bonds, the maid after the silk shawl that she had bought with her wages. Everyone ran to collect the thing he or she prized most highly.

And the little goblin did so, too. In a bound or two, he was up the stairs and in the room of the student, who was standing quite calmly at the open window, looking out at the fire in the house across the road. The goblin seized the wonderful book from the table, put it in his scarlet cap, and hugged it with both arms. The most precious thing in the house was saved! Then he rushed up to the roof, right to the top of the chimney stack, and there he sat, lit up by the flames of the house on fire over the way, still firmly clasping the red cap with the treasure inside.

Now he knew where his heart lay. Student? Grocer? His choice was clear.

But when the fire had been put out, and the goblin had had time to think more calmly. "Well . . . I'll divide my time between them," he decided. "I can't quite give up the grocer, because of the porridge."

Just like a human, really. We, too, like to keep on good terms with the grocer, because of the porridge. ᷐

207

Translation, compilation, and introductions copyright © 2004 by Naomi Lewis
Illustrations copyright © 2004 by Joel Stewart

First U.S. edition 2004

Library of Congress Cataloging-in-Publication Data

Andersen, H. C. (Hans Christian), 1805–1875.
Tales of Hans Christian Andersen / translated and introduced by Naomi Lewis ; illustrated by Joel Stewart. — 1st U.S. ed.
p. cm.
Contents: The princess and the pea — The tinderbox — Thumbelina — The emperor's new clothes —
The little mermaid — The steadfast tin soldier — The wild swans — The flying trunk — The ugly duckling —
The nightingale — The snow queen — The little match girl — The goblin at the grocer's.
ISBN 0-7636-2515-9
1. Fairy tales — Denmark. 2. Children's stories, Danish — Translations into English. [1. Fairy tales. 2. Short stories.]
I. Lewis, Naomi. II. Stewart, Joel, ill. III. Title.
PZ8.A54 2004
839.8'136[Fic] — dc22   2004045171

2 4 6 8 10 9 7 5 3 1

Printed in China

This book was typeset in Minion Condensed.
The illustrations were digitally created.

Candlewick Press
2067 Massachusetts Avenue
Cambridge, Massachusetts 02140

visit us at www.candlewick.com